BOY UNDERWATER

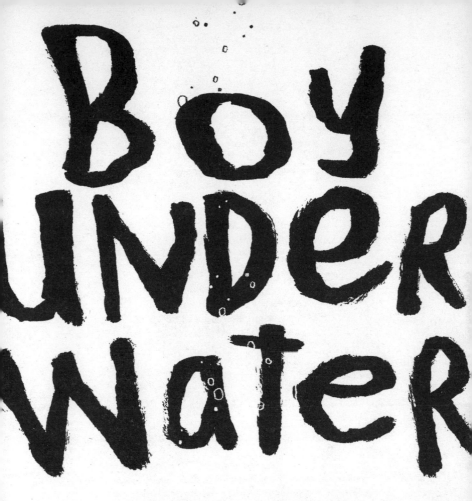

BOY UNDER WATER

ADAM BARON

(Franklin, Vi and Frieda's dad —
you know, the one who coaches Year Four football)

HarperCollins *Children's Books*

First published in Great Britain by
HarperCollins *Children's Books* in 2018
HarperCollins *Children's Books* is a division of
HarperCollins*Publishers* Ltd,
HarperCollins Publishers
1 London Bridge Street
London SE1 9GF

The HarperCollins website address is:
www.harpercollins.co.uk

3

ISBN 978-0-00-826701-8

Typeset in Sabon 11/18pt
Printed and bound in England by CPI Group (UK) Ltd, Croydon CR0 4YY

Almost all of this novel is dedicated to
Ben and Ollie Robinson.

The first line of page thirty-eight is
for their parents, though.

CHAPTER ONE

Here's something you won't believe.

I, Cymbeline Igloo, have never been swimming.

It's the swimming bit you won't believe, by the way, though if you don't believe my name either, it really *is* Cymbeline Igloo, and you have to believe that because it's written on my schoolbag and in my jumpers and on lots of other things, like my passport. You won't believe I've never been swimming because I mean totally never. Not *ever*. Not once, in my whole life. I am nine years old! I am the third-best footballer in Year 4 (joint) and the second-best at roller-skating after Elizabeth Fisher and she goes to a club on Sundays. I am fit and healthy and totally normal in every way (apart from my name) but I have never set foot in the sea, a river or a lake, not to mention an actual, normal, everyday swimming pool.

Not in my life.

Until last Monday.

I blame my mum. Totally. She's just never taken me. Not as a baby, not as a toddler, not when I was at nursery or when I was in Key Stage One. When I've asked why, she's come up with rubbish excuse after even *more* rubbish excuse. We don't go to the beach because she's allergic to sand. Rivers, *she says*, are where crocodiles live (we live in south-east London). Lakes, she *tells* me, are like lochs, which could contain things like the Loch Ness monster, which is so dangerous (not) that no one has ever actually SEEN IT (sorry, Scotland, but it's true: your monster is rubbish).

As for swimming pools, chlorine (what's that?) can make you itchy and you often find clumps of other people's hair in swimming pools and some of it doesn't come from their heads but from *other places*.

That last bit is actually the most convincing argument for staying away from the whole swimming thing, though it's still not good enough and Mum SHOULD HAVE TAKEN ME. This is something that was made spectacularly clear last Monday when something happened that I can only describe as . . .

A COMPLETE AND TOTAL DISASTER.

'*Line up, everyone. Chop-chop, hurry along now.*'

That was Miss Phillips. *Last Monday.* Before I tell you about her, though, I think I'd better answer a question that has probably popped up in your head like toast. Surely, I hear you think, if my mum refused to take me swimming, then my dad could have taken me instead. I sometimes forget that most people have two parents, something you mostly only ever really see at parents' evening, or the school play. A mum and, next to her, a dad. Looking bored or checking his phone. My best friend Lance, who is joint third-best footballer in Year 4 with me, actually has FOUR parents, because his mum and dad split up and then married other people, who are now his step-mum and step-dad.

This of course is not fair, as it means he's got

three more parents than me, something that is true because my dad died when I was one and I don't remember him. He's just pictures on the mantelpiece and the reason Mum starts crying sometimes. Christmas Day. My birthday, especially. Wail wail, sob sob. I mean, I do feel sorry for her but it doesn't exactly help if you're really trying to enjoy your new Lego.

So no dad to take me swimming to make up for the fact that my *mum* simply *never has*.

'Have we all got our togs?'

'Togs, Miss?' Lance asked.

'Swimming things. Towel, goggles, costume.'

'*Costume?*'

'Trunks, in your case, Lance. Not sure a bikini would suit you. Well? Cymbeline, have you got yours? You look a little pale.'

'Yes, Miss,' I said, my voice sounding a bit funny.

'Right then. It's only a short walk. Keep up, everyone.'

And off we went. To the swimming pool.

This was *last Monday*, though before I fill you in on that I'd better take another step back to the week before, which I'm really sorry about but I've just started to realise that this telling-stories gig is HARD. Miss Phillips again, the Friday before last Monday:

'Children, you'll be dismayed to hear that we won't be doing any more RE on Monday mornings.'

Once the cheering died down, Lance asked why not.

'Because, Lance – finger out, please – we'll be starting swimming lessons.'

'*We?*' Danny Jones asked, quite a lot of fear in his voice.

'I mean you. I'll be watching.'

The relief at not having to see Miss Phillips in a swimsuit was almost overwhelming. Everyone started chatting with excitement and Lance turned and grinned at me.

'I wonder if we'll be joint third best at swimming too.'

'I . . .'

'What is it, Cym? You look . . . Are you all right?'

'Yes of course. But I don't think we'll be joint good any more. Not at swimming, Lance.'

'What? Oh no. I bet you're *really* great at it, aren't you, Cym?'

'Er,' I said. 'Well.' And then I said, and I don't know WHY I said it, 'Yeah, I'm like really epic at swimming.'

'I bet you're not as good as me, Igloo,' said Billy Lee, checking that Miss Phillips wasn't looking before elbowing me in the stomach. Billy Lee does that. *Always*. He's a super-horror is Billy, sort of like a purple Minion but there's nothing you can do to make him go back yellow. 'I can do butterfly,' he went on. 'Can you do butterfly?'

'Yeah,' I said. 'Course.'

'And what else?'

'Er . . .' I thought hard.

'Well?'

'Moth?'

'*What?*'

'I can do that. Moth. As well as . . . butterfly,' I said.

Lance cracked up at that and slapped me on the back, though I don't know why. *Butterfly?* I thought we were going swimming, not out in the park to wave nets about. I hid my ignorance, though, and stared at Billy Lee's flat smirking face as he said, 'Right, we'll see about that. Monday morning, me and you, Igloo.'

'What?'

'A swimming race. Crawl.'

'I thought you said "swimming".'

'The stroke crawl, dib-head.'

'Of course,' I said. And by the end of lunchtime it was all around the class. I, Cymbeline Igloo (likeable, friendly, supportive classmate to all), would be taking on Billy Lee (brash, snide, downright bully when he can get away with it) at a *SWIMMING RACE* at Lewisham Pool.

'The loser's a total dib-head,' Billy Lee said, but I felt like one of those already.

Me, in a *swimming* race? When I had never, not once, EVER been swimming, and against someone a foot taller than me whose parents signed him up for *every sport going*? What – bangheadondesk – was – bangheadondesk – I – bangheadondesk – thinking? I kept asking myself that all day, racking my brains for some way out of it, desperate until something amazing happened. It was home time. I was in the playground. Just standing there when . . .

VERONIQUE CHANG CAME RIGHT UP TO ME.

Veronique does not come up to people. Not even Miss Phillips, whose grammar and spelling she is often known to correct. Miss Phillips thanks her when she does this but I don't think she really means it. Veronique's this rare unapproachable genius. She can spell words like 'piculear' and 'sircumstanz'. Her mum's French so she can speak that and her dad's Chinese so she can also speak . . . Satsuma (I think that's what it is). Or is it Tangerine? Never mind. She's FIVE whole GRADES ahead of me at piano (she's on Grade Five). And she's . . . No one's looking, right? I can say it . . .

REALLY PRETTY. She's got this long black hair that's so glossy you can almost see your own face in it and she smells like someone somewhere is eating candyfloss.

I was so psyched by Veronique just coming up like that, that I forgot how I'd managed to get myself into the worst situation of my entire life. Until, that is, she spoke, and my insides slopped over like a badly cooked pancake.

'Cymbeline, I really hope you win.'

'Sorry?'

'On Monday. Against Billy. He lives near us and

he's *such* an idiot. I hope you smash him,' she said, smiling at me.

When I didn't answer, Veronique gave me an odd look and walked off, after which my mum appeared out of the crowd and started to interfere with my hair.

'Did you have a good day, Champ?'

'Yes, Mum,' I answered. 'Perfect. I spent it thinking about how you are, without doubt, the best mother in the entire world.'

'Ah . . .'

'NOT!'

'Cymbeline? Cym? Is there something wrong?'

'Nothing YOU can fix,' I said, and stomped over to the gate, where Billy Lee was smirking at me.

'See you on Monday,' he said.

CHAPTER TWO

Google search: how to crawl.

Result: baby may spend time rocking forwards and backwards initially but by between eight and twelve months she should be crawling confidently and pulling herself upright.

What? A *baby* can do it and I can't? No, wait, that's not swimming crawling, is it?

Google search: how to *swim* crawl.

Right, here we go. That looks doable. Swimwell.org says you have to lie in the water face down and move your arms like two windmills. You tilt your head from side to side to breathe. Fine. How hard can it be?

Shut computer.

'Mum!' I called from the living room.

'Yes, Cym?'

'I need to have a bath!'

I heard a teacup smash on the kitchen floor before she came rushing through.

'Cym, are you okay? Are you feeling all right?'

'Yes, why?'

'It's just that, well, you *asked* to have a bath.'

'I know, I, er . . . I just feel that being clean is very important.'

'Of course. Well, I'm glad you've finally woken up to that. But won't a shower do?'

'Not on this occasion, no.'

Upstairs, I ran a bath and began. Head down, bottom up. I probably shouldn't have added the bubble bath, though. Pretty soon I was rubbing my eyes and spitting out mouthfuls of foam. The problem was that it just wasn't deep or long enough. Or wide enough. My arms hit the sides when I tried to windmill them and I kept banging my head on the end. Swimwell.org had mentioned something called tumble-turns, for swapping round and going the other way. But when I tried one of those I pulled the plug out with my big toe and kicked the bubble bath out of the window.

'Have you gone mad?!' Mum screamed, running

in. There was more water out of the bath than in it.

'At least I'm clean,' I said. Whereupon Mum just shook her head and picked up the shampoo bottle.

'Eyes,' she said.

I turned round and let her wash my hair without complaining (much) and when she finished I asked what we were doing that weekend.

'What would you like to do?'

'Can we . . .?'

'Yes, Cym?'

'Go swimming?'

Mum went quiet. Then she said, 'Well, we'll see. Perhaps. Though I was thinking of taking you to Charlton tomorrow afternoon. Early birthday present.'

'Seriously?'

Charlton is our local team and the side I will be playing for one day. I'll be the captain, like Johnnie Jackson is now, though I'll have to share it with Lance of course as we're equal. Danny Jones (second best) and Billy Lee (best, grrrr) will be playing for Chelsea in the Premier League so I don't have to worry about them. The thought of going was brilliant, especially as, being an EARLY birthday present, I would surely get my other special treat AS WELL (more on that later).

I thought about my birthday. The fact it was still a whole massive week away was almost like torture. Funny, isn't it, that the nearer your birthday gets the more it seems like it's never *actually* going to come?

'Thanks, Mum! Did you get tickets?'

'Not yet. I only just thought of it. I'll go online in a bit. They don't sell out.'

'Fab. What about Sunday afternoon?'

'For what?'

'Swimming.'

'Are they open on Sunday? No, I don't think they are.'

'Oh. Well, maybe not Charlton then this weekend. Perhaps we could go next week instead . . .'

But Mum wasn't listening. She got me out, plonked a towel over my head, and hurried downstairs. By the time I got there she was smiling up from the computer.

'Got them,' she said. 'West Upper Stand, your favourite.'

'Thanks, Mum,' I said.

That night, after tea, Mum let me stay up with her and we curled up on the sofa watching the first *Harry Potter*. I like Harry Potter as much as anyone but there's something no one else seems to think about when they're banging on about wanting a Firebolt or how they wish they could apparate. He's got no mum or dad. They're dead. I don't think about my dad much, but sometimes it's like he sort of thinks about me, makes me remember that he's not there. That he's dead. It happens when I read stories like *Harry Potter*. I don't wish I had a super-fast broomstick or that I could move around in a magic way. I just wish I had photos like Harry has. That move. Then the man on the mantelpiece might mean a bit more to me. He might feel like my dad, not just some bloke in a checked shirt with his arm round someone who looks like she must be my mum's younger sister.

Also, Harry Potter knows what happened to his dad but whenever I ask about mine everyone says it's not something I need to think about until I'm older (like offside). Lance asked me once and I was a bit embarrassed to admit I didn't know so I just told him he got ill.

'And I don't suppose they had Calpol then, did they?' Lance said.

When the film finished I expected Mum to tell me it was bedtime. I even started to get up from the sofa but she just smiled and asked if I wanted to see the second one. I didn't ask why we were getting to watch *two films in a row*. I just nodded and we watched it all, though I could hardly stay awake.

When it was over she carried me up and I saw that the clock in the hall said half past eleven. I'd only stayed up that late once before, last year at Uncle Bill and Auntie Mill's joint 'significant' birthday. It was half ten when I woke up in the morning and nearly midday by the time Mum had got the pancakes made and we'd eaten them.

'What about the pool, Mum?' I said, when I couldn't stuff any more in.

She looked up at the clock and sighed. 'Sorry, love, don't think we'd get there and back before kick-off, do you?'

I didn't answer. There wasn't any point. She just wasn't going to take me. I started to get mad but, when I looked up, Mum had tears in her eyes and she was staring at me. I saw her swallow and then move towards me, her soft arms going round my neck.

'I love you,' she said, and I believed it so much I didn't mind about the swimming. Not then, at least, though on Monday it was different, believe me. In the meantime, though, I had Charlton to look forward to:

come on, you Addicks! It was great, which meant my real birthday trip was going to be epic. We got chips and Mum let me have a battered sausage. I heard three swear words, one of which was completely new to me but, somehow, I still knew it was a swear word. We were drawing with Rotherham 1–1 when Johnnie Jackson scored a header in the last minute. Yes! That would have been me, not Lance. He's good at doing crosses but he runs away from headers and pretends not to at the last moment, when the ball's already on the ground. I might be a bit better than him, actually.

'How's this term shaping up?' Mum asked on Sunday night. We'd been up in town all day doing art workshops at the National Gallery. Mum's an artist and this is one of her jobs. She talks about a picture to kids, then takes them off to a different room to do some art based on it. I don't mind. I like drawing and making things, but what I really like is watching Mum talking. I like watching everyone else listening to her. I saw a man there who'd been before. In fact, he'd been the last five weeks with his two little girls. He spent a long time talking to Mum about the pictures and he really thanked her a lot at the end. One of the little girls grabbed hold of my leg and wouldn't let go. I pretended to mind but she was cute, actually.

'This term? 'S all right.'

'But what are you going to be doing?' Mum asked. 'I missed the meeting about it because I was working and they haven't emailed the list through yet.'

'Romans,' I said. 'And something called reproduction. Miss Phillips said we're not allowed to be embarrassed when we do that but she went red when she said it so I think I'm going to be.'

'Oh well. Anything else new?'

Children, you'll be dismayed to hear that we won't be doing any more RE on Monday mornings.

'Nothing worth talking about,' I said.

CHAPTER THREE

'Cymbeline. William. IGLOO. There is *NOTHING* wrong with you at *ALL*. Get out of bed, *RIGHT NOW.*'

'But I'm ill!'

'No. You. Are. Not. You have no temperature and your throat is completely normal.'

'It's *not*. It *huuuu-rrrrts*. It –'

'Cymbeline, we've talked about this. If you miss a day of school, you have to be *properly* ill. I've got Messy Art today; if I miss it to look after you, I don't get paid. Simple.'

Messy Art is something Mum does with toddlers in a church hall on Monday mornings. In the holidays I have to go too and the one thing I'd say is that Mum is *pants* at naming things. Messy Art should be called 'Messy Miniature Lunatics Go Ape'. But when she mentioned it I sighed. I know how hard Mum works and how we need every penny we have. She does sums on bits of paper at the start of every month. I found them once and looked down the columns. I'm okay at sums and it didn't take long to work out that, after all the food and dinner money and the gas and electric and the council tax and a bit for school shoes she was saving up for and a fair few other things that didn't sound like much fun, my mum had exactly nine pounds forty-three pence left over. There wasn't anything on the list that *she* might have wanted.

'Up!' she shouted, and I just sighed.

The first thing I noticed was the smell. Tangy, in my nose. Then the sound. As soon as Miss Phillips pushed the door of the leisure centre open I could hear it: loud and echoey and not quite real, laughter and voices and a hosepipe going, a phone ringing. It was weird but no one else seemed to notice it. But I gawped at the high ceiling and the bright light; it was like walking into a big dream. Then, as we marched through the foyer, I saw shapes moving around on the other side of these MASSIVE windows. And that's when I first saw it: the *pool*.

My stomach lurched. Sweat prickled on my forehead. I stopped dead still and someone bashed into me from behind and knocked me over. I picked myself up and just stared through the glass at the huge blue expanse shimmering in front of me. My eyes went big as Frisbees and I knew: I couldn't do it. No. Way. I'd just have to tell Miss Phillips. Confess. I shook my head, not even sure that I could take another step forward until I saw who had knocked me over.

'Sorry, Cymbeline,' said Veronique, pushing her hair to the side of her face as she leaned in close to me. Veronique was smiling again and I smiled back as I realised something. Her breath smelled of Weetabix. It's exactly what *I* have for breakfast! We were made for each other! When she wished me good luck I mumbled thanks, and then followed everyone else through the turnstiles.

'Boys, left,' Miss Phillips trilled. 'Girls, this way please. No messing about now, boys.'

Now I know – as you see me walk into the changing rooms – what you are thinking. Clever as you are (and you must be clever to have chosen this book) you have worked out that my mum, not ever having taken me swimming, is unlikely to have bought me any swimming trunks. Especially as, unlike Billy Lee's parents, she is not 'rolling in it'. On Friday, Miss Phillips had told us that if we forgot to bring trunks then we would have to wear the school spares, and the ones she held up brought howls of laughter: an ancient bodysuit, suitable, she said, for girls *or* boys. There was no way I was wearing that, but what could I do?

I got the idea on Saturday but it wasn't until Sunday night that I could act. Mum goes to bed really early on Sundays, hardly any later than me. After she kissed me goodnight I lay awake as she watched a bit of telly downstairs and then listened to a few records. Old slow ones that she plays ALL THE TIME. I listened as she then sat in silence for a bit, until her phone rang. She chatted to someone and then I heard her lock the front door and the back door, before she went in the bathroom. When she went into her bedroom I waited a long time, listening. And there's something about my mum that I would like you to keep to yourself. She snores, and when I heard her doing this I got out of bed, opened my door and tiptoed down the hall to the boxroom.

The boxroom is a small room near the bathroom. I don't go in there much. It's not that I'm not allowed; I just don't. There's nothing for me, just boring stuff that Mum stores. There's a tennis racket that she never plays with and some old bottles of wine. She doesn't drink. There's a pair of weightlifting weights and bin bags full of clothes. Uncle Bill bought me a Scalextric on eBay and it's a pain to keep putting up and down. The boxroom would be perfect for it but whenever I ask Mum why she doesn't chuck that junk away she just smiles and interferes with my hair. She doesn't answer, but I know why she keeps it all.

It's my dad's stuff.

Snore, snore, snore, whistle. Snore, SNORE. I glanced back at Mum's door and then I turned the handle. It only took five minutes to find the swimming trunks. They were in the second bag I opened (the first had baby clothes in, a little odd as Mum normally sells all my old stuff on eBay). There were even some goggles. I snuck them into my schoolbag with a towel and went to bed.

'Right, boys,' Miss Phillips said, putting her head round the changing-room door. 'Come on now.'

'Yes, Miss,' we all said, apart from Marcus Breen of course. Being Marcus Breen, he stuck his willy between his legs and told Miss Phillips he thought he was in the wrong changing room.

Have you got a Marcus Breen in your class?

We all filed out, a rushing noise getting louder as we made our way across these bumpy white tiles. We passed an old man having a shower who was completely covered in black and white hair, like a badger with a person's head on, and then a group of big ladies approaching the water like some hippos I'd seen on the Discovery Channel. We stopped right by the edge of the pool and Miss Phillips chatted to a young man in shorts and a red polo shirt, with this big chin like a deck of cards. He looked down at us as she spoke to him, nodding all the time. Then he started to speak. He told us about safety things, the importance of swimming, how we had to listen to his whistle and do exactly what he said. He went on and on, while I looked at the pool. The smell was stronger now, biting into my nostrils. Our bit went from the deep end, where we were standing, towards the shallow end. The rest was portioned off by fat plastic rope things and was being used by the big ladies, who were jumping up and down to music. I began to think – yes! – this is going to be it for the first lesson, *just talking*. Until the man said, 'Now then, which of you has never had any proper swimming lessons before?'

I fixed my eyes on him and took a big, deep breath. This was my chance. I could just raise my hand and admit it. I'd *never* been swimming. I could tell Billy Lee I'd been winding him up on Friday. I could join all the other beginners and finally learn to swim. I was pretty sure I'd be fairly good at it if I was shown how. I'm good at sport. I may not have told you, but I'm third-best footballer in Year 4 (joint). In a few weeks I'd be ready to take anyone on, including Billy Lee. But there was a problem. There *were* no other first-time learners. Not one other person put their hand up. Not even Marcus Breen.

'Impressive,' the man said. 'Well, let's start at the other end of things. If you've all had lessons, has anyone here passed Level Four?'

'I have,' shouted Lance, sticking his armpit in my

face as he shoved his hand up. Belvedere Blatt said he had too, and so did Laura Pinter and Elizabeth Fisher (though she just needed a wee).

'Great,' the man said, nodding. 'Well, you'll be our demonstrators. If you could just slide into the pool please, and –'

'But I've passed Level FIVE,' barked a voice from right behind me.

It was of course Billy Lee. He strode to the front and put his hands on his hips, the jet-black goggles strapped on to his forehead making him look like a giant bug. Everyone else sort of shrank back from him – apart from the teacher that is, who nodded admiringly. He asked Billy if he could dive and Billy said of course. The man nodded again and I could tell something: Billy had forgotten about our race. He was so intent on showing off that he didn't care about it. The man stepped to the side as Billy put his goggles over his eyes. He did this elaborate stretch with his arms, and then hooked his toes over the last tile near the edge. He would have dived in if Lance hadn't called out,

'Wait!'

My friend. My so-called BEST friend. Billy

would have spent the entire lesson demonstrating his incredible skills. He'd have forgotten about me. I could have plonked about in the shallow end until it was time to go.

BUT NO!

'Please, sir,' Lance shouted, 'Cymbeline's got Level Five too!'

'Cymbeline?' the man said, looking around at all the girls. I get that A LOT.

'Here,' Lance said, pushing me forward. 'He's EPIC at swimming.'

A hush developed. Everyone looked at me. Most of the class looked at me with expectation. The swimming teacher looked at me as if he *very* much doubted what Lance had said and Billy Lee looked at me with what I can only describe as a hideous, terrible glee. Because he'd realised. He'd either found out somehow, or he could just tell by looking at me, but he knew: I was not epic at swimming. And not only that. He could tell that I'd never been swimming *at all*.

'Yeah,' he said, holding up his hands and stepping behind me. 'Don't ask me, sir. Ask Cym. He's incredible. He can do butterfly. He can even do some other strokes I've never heard of. Moth, wasn't it? You should demonstrate, shouldn't you? Show us all how it's done, Cym. GO ON!'

And I felt two hands on my back. Billy's hands. And then I found myself moving.

Forward.

And then I felt myself F L Y I N G.

CHAPTER FOUR

Swimwell.org has quite a bit to say about diving. It is, says Swimwell.org, the action of 'leaping or springing into water'. I had not, however, paid much attention to this part of their website as I really hadn't thought that, on our very first school lesson, we'd be doing that. So, when I entered the water below me, it wasn't with a dive so much as a sort of tangled upside-down *ouch*. Water, as I found out then, HURTS. I blame the pain for what happened next. After the initial shock, I did not panic. No. I put the knowledge I had learned on Swimwell.org to use. I started to move my arms like windmills, just like the woman in the pictures had done. I started to move my head from side to side.

Both of these things *should* have sent me bulleting to the other end of the pool, where I would have been able to execute a perfect tumble-turn (minus bubble bath). For some reason this did not happen, something I intend to inform Swimwell.org about in the strongest possible terms.

I did not, as they said I would, go forward. Instead, to my intense surprise, I went down, entering what seemed like another world in which you couldn't really hear anything. Everything was blue and when I looked around I saw bolts of white light whipping round. I saw legs wiggling across the pool, and then I saw something else. It was, I realised, the bottom of the pool, and it was coming towards me. Fast. And then I felt it, with my head, after which I felt sort of floaty and not particularly concerned that I was now at the bottom of a swimming pool. At least I'd done it – I was swimming, though not how most people do it, I admit. Then I felt something else, a sort of emptiness around my waist that I couldn't quite understand. I was about to investigate when I heard the

It really did sound like an explosion. It came from above and I looked up to see a mass of bubbles and foam coming towards me, out of which two hands appeared, which hooked themselves under my armpits. Then I felt myself rising, up out of this quiet new world, sound suddenly smashing back into my ears as I hit the surface. What happened next is the COMPLETE AND TOTAL DISASTER that I was talking about before. My rescuer pushed me up against the side and, as I held on to the edge and gasped, I looked up, confused. For there was the man in the red shirt. He was standing above me with a long pole in his hand. Miss Phillips was there too, bending over and looking horrified.

So who had jumped in to get me? Billy Lee? It must have been. And I'd never live it down, not EVER. But Billy was standing at the back with his mouth wide open. Everyone was there except . . .

It was only when I turned to the left that I saw who it was who'd rescued me.

Veronique Chang.

I found out later that Veronique's on Level 9, or whatever it is that lets you swim for the borough at the national finals. She'd just climbed out of the water and was grabbing my arm to pull me out. Seeing her do that, Miss Phillips reached forward for the other one.

'NO!' I screamed, spitting out water like a stone fish in a fountain. 'Please don't pull me ou—'

But it was too late. My legs kicking, I left the swimming pool, though not quite as I'd entered it. Earlier, I'd tied the cord on my dad's swimming trunks as tight as I possibly could. But it wasn't quite tight enough.

'I can see his willy! I CAN SEE HIS WILLY!'

Marcus Breen. That was him. And if you haven't got one in your class you can have ours.

You can come and get him, ANY TIME.

CHAPTER FIVE

'Hello,' I said when I got home later. I was talking on the phone to a man from British Airways. 'May I book two tickets to Australia, please?'

'Er, yes,' the man said, possibly taken aback by my young-sounding voice. 'When would you like to travel, sir?'

'Today, please.'

'Oh. Right. And which city do you want to go to in Australia?'

'Which . . .?'

'Brisbane, Sydney, Melbourne or Perth?'

I hadn't thought about that. 'Which one is the furthest away from St Saviour's School, Blackheath, Lewisham?'

'I don't know, sir. It's not a question I've ever been asked before.'

'Oh. Okay then, how about this? Which of them, do you think, is the least likely to EVER be visited by someone from St Saviour's School, Blackheath, Lewisham? I mean, like, NEVER?'

I never heard the man's answer, so I can't tell you what it was. My mum came in and saw me with her bank card in my hand. I thought she'd be mad but she just gave me a soft smile and pressed the red button on the phone before putting it down on the kitchen table. Then she interfered with my hair.

'Australia, hey? A holiday?'

I looked at her. 'No. We're going to live there.'

'Really?'

'Yes, though I thought about France first.'

'France?'

'Because of the chocolate croissants. But it's too near. Rachel Jones went there on holiday last summer. She still bangs on about it. She might see me.'

'And you don't speak French.'

'I know. So that's why I thought of Australia. It's the furthest country from us for one thing, but I saw an Australian cricketer on the telly last week.

He was speaking English. Sort of.'

'Right,' Mum said, and I thought she was going to laugh for some reason. But the trembling of her lips didn't turn into laughter. She was staring at me, hard, and then she reached out to take my hand. She was wearing her red jumper, the really itchy one, and the sleeve scratched against my wrist. She tried to mouth some words.

'Sorry,' she said. 'Cymbeline, I'm sorry I never took you swimming. I really am. I'm so, so sorry.'

And so she should have been! And I nearly said that. But what she did then stopped me. I've told you about her crying, haven't I? But she'd never cried like this before. I thought crying was done with your eyes mostly, and your mouth a bit. But when Mum started to cry it was with all of her. Her shoulders moved up and down and her throat made this weird croaking noise. Soon her whole body was shaking, like the washing machine when it's nearly finished, and all I could do was watch her. She kept saying *sorry, sorry*, over and over, or at least she tried to because she couldn't get the word out properly. She clutched her stomach and shook, my wrist really itching now, but unlike the washing machine she didn't slow down and go quiet again. She carried on, and on, and *on*, trying to say sorry, and I heard myself say it's okay, it's okay, it was nothing really, just the whole class seeing my willy after the best girl in the entire world had seen me floundering around and dragged me out of the swimming pool. Don't *worry* about it. But Mum didn't seem to be able to hear me. It was like – and this may sound weird – she wasn't saying sorry to *me* at all. But someone else. It was like there was someone else there, with us in the kitchen.

Mum shook, and she shook, and I couldn't make her hear me. There was nothing I could do, so eventually I took my hand back and went upstairs to my bedroom. It was quiet in there. Everything was really still. I took a Lego model to bits and put it back together again, though it didn't look quite the same. I got an Asterix from the shelf, but for the first time *ever* nothing inside it made me laugh. Not even Obelix. So I just sat there, snizzling Mr Fluffy, until I heard footsteps on the stairs. But they went past, and I heard Mum's bedroom door opening. And closing. I walked out on to the landing and listened, but I couldn't hear anything. So through the door I said, 'Mum?'

There was no answer. I tried again.

'*Mum?*'

'Oh,' she said from the other side of the door. 'Hi, Cymbeline. Listen, champ, I'm not feeling very well, okay?'

'Oh. Can I get you anything?'

'No, that's all right, love. A bit of a headache. I put a pizza in the oven. Is it okay if you take it out when the bell goes and have it for supper?'

'On my own?'

'Yes, love.'

'All right,' I said.

'You know how to do that, don't you?'

'With oven gloves.'

'And turn the oven off. Then there's ice cream in the freezer. Remember to push the little door shut tight, won't you?'

'Okay.'

'And then . . .'

'Yes, Mum?'

'Can you tuck yourself up into bed? Clean your teeth first.'

'All right.'

'And I'll come out then and give you a kiss goodnight.'

'All right,' I said again. She never did, though. I

40

left the pizza in too long and it was black round the edges. I ate the middle. The ice-cream tub was wedged into the freezer compartment so tightly that I couldn't pull it out. I had a yoghurt instead. And two chocolate biscuits. And another two chocolate biscuits. And a small packet of Haribos. I cleaned my teeth and had a wee, even though Mum hadn't reminded me to do that, and then I had just one more chocolate biscuit. And then I cleaned my teeth again and lay in bed waiting for her. She always kisses me goodnight. Always, even if I've done something I perhaps, *maybe*, should not have, and she's just spent half an hour doing LOUD at me.

But not that night.

I called out for her, and then went out on to the landing and knocked on her door. She didn't answer. Or come out.

I went back to bed, sure that I'd never fall asleep, though I did in the end. I know that because I had a dream, a really horrible one, like what had happened to me that day, though the water wasn't blue and shiny but brown and dirty and cold, and it went in my throat and eyes and I was turning over and over until I was spat out awake. It was terrible, believe me, though

nothing compared to waking up the next morning.
That was way worse, because of what I found out then.

My mum wasn't crying any more.

And she wasn't shut up in her bedroom.

My mum was gone.

CHAPTER SIX

Lance once asked me a question. We were in the hall doing PE, something I'd been looking forward to all week, but which turned out to be *terrible*. We were starting Year 3 then with Mr Ashe, who I happen to know is a *boss* footballer. He coaches the Year 6 team and we sometimes interrupt our Year 4 Saturday-morning training to watch their matches. Before every game he does kick-ups and catches the ball on the back of his neck while the Year 6 kids all groan. So I thought PE would be a chance to improve and perhaps even overtake Danny Jones. But it wasn't. That term, Mr Ashe explained, as we lined up near the wall bars, we would not be doing football. Or rugby. Not even netball, which would at least have involved a ball.

Instead we were going to be doing *gymnastics*, and if you don't think that's terrible it means you are probably a girl (though if you're not, BIG SORRY AND RESPECT). The girls all squealed with delight, and soon I could see why.

Now I have to admit something. I like girls as much as the next boy, and maybe a little bit more, but I'd always thought that when it came to sport girls just weren't *quite* as good. That day I found out that I was wrong. Hardly had the words left Mr Ashe's lips than I was staring in mouth-wide amazement as girl after girl did the most incredible things. Laura Pinter did a cartwheel that was just like a real wheel going round, especially when she kept going and did three in a row. Rachel Jones then did another one but sort of twisted round halfway in the air so that she ended up on two feet, facing the way she'd come, her arms pointing up to the ceiling.

Wow! It looked so easy but when I tried I just got tangled up. The other boys were the same, looking like rejects from a toy factory, the ones that didn't work right. The girls were smug too, standing up straighter than they normally did and raising their chins as they walked back to start again. In contrast, our own rubbish-ness was sort of humiliating, though there was one moment I did enjoy. Vi Delap did this thing that I simply COULD NOT believe. She stood straight and bent over backwards, reaching up and behind her. In less than a second she'd put her hands on the floor into a bridge, and then flicked her feet over so that she was standing up again. Billy Lee saw her and tried himself. The very loud echo, when his head connected with the wooden floor, is still one of my Top Five Sounds Of All Time.

'Cymbeline,' Lance said, sitting down beside me and rubbing his elbow. And his knee. And then his bum. He looked miserable, though I didn't think it came from the gymnastics. 'Where did you get your name from?'

'My name?'

'Yeah. I mean, I always thought it was normal because it's what you're called, isn't it?'

'So why don't you think it's normal now?'

'Well, my dad –'

'Wait, Lance. Is this your dad-dad you mean, or your new-dad?'

'My new-dad. I told him you were my best friend and he thought you were a girl. When I told him you

45

weren't, he laughed a bit and told me he'd never heard that name before and it must be because I went to 'that kind of school'. He didn't tell me what 'that kind of school' was because my mum came in. So where did you get it from?'

'I could ask you the same thing.'

'I suppose,' Lance said. 'Though my name's not as weird as yours. I've never met another Cymbeline but there's another Lance in this school. And another kid called Lance in me and my dad's cycling club.'

'Your dad-dad?'

'My dad-dad.'

'But still, if you ask me, I can ask you. Why are you called Lance?'

'I'm not allowed to tell you.'

'*What?*'

'It's my dad,' Lance explained.

'Your dad-dad?'

'Yeah, my dad-dad. He says I shouldn't say. Or, if I *do* say, I have to say that it's just a random name. I'm definitely not named after Lance Armstrong.'

'Lance who?'

'Never mind. But why are you called Cymbeline?'

'Because of my dad,' I said.

'Your dead-dad?'

'Yeah.'

'Was he called Cymbeline?'

'No, his own parents did not inflict that on him. His name was David.'

'So . . .?'

'Mum says he was an actor and that when she met him he was in this play by Shakespeare. *Cymbeline*. So they called me it.'

'What's the play about?'

'No idea.'

'You never asked your mum?'

'Yes, and she told me. She even took me to see it.'

'Well then.'

'Have you *seen* Shakespeare? I've still no idea. It was impossible to understand and anyway we didn't stay to the end.'

'Why not?'

'There's this line in it. "Fear no more the heat of the sun." It comes when there are people on the ground who are dead but you can still see them breathing. When this king dude said the line my mum just grabbed my hand and pulled me out of the theatre and took me home.'

I didn't tell Lance that, once again, she'd cried when she'd done that. She cried all the way back. She put me to bed and the tears rolled into my hair as she clung on to me.

'I hate my name,' Lance said, as Marcus Breen did a forward roll into the piano.

'Why?'

'It's Lance . . . who I can't mention. He was a cycling hero but now he's this super giant cheater, and I've got to wear his name forever.'

'I know how you feel,' I'd said, though now, waking up, it wasn't my name that bothered me. That was a burden I'd always had to carry. Now there was something bigger, heavier, and I couldn't get away from it. My dad. You'd think being dead would be the best way to leave someone alone, wouldn't you? But my dad being dead was something even more real than if he'd been alive. It never used to feel like that, but now it did. And my mum felt it too. I could see that. My dad being dead was so big for her, a huge thing. It was so heavy that she couldn't put it down. And so heavy that she didn't have the strength to carry me any more, as well as it.

* * *

Uncle Bill was sitting on my bed when I woke up the next morning. He was smiling, but only with his mouth. The rest of him wasn't smiling at all.

CHAPTER SEVEN

I blinked, amazed and delighted to see Bill, as he's loads of fun, though at first I was worried that he'd see Mr Fluffy. At school I deny the existence of Mr Fluffy, something I have to apologise to him for later. When Lance comes round for sleepovers I hide him underneath my pillow. Lance has got a purple cat that I pretend not to see when he shoves it down his sleeping bag.

Fortunately Mr Fluffy was out of sight somewhere, probably beneath the duvet, though that didn't make me feel any less worried. Uncle Bill's expression was weird. And we only ever see him at weekends – so what was he doing here *now*?

'Where's Mum?' I said.

Uncle Bill scratched his beard. It's black, with this little clump of white below his mouth, like he's been eating a cream cake. You keep wanting to wipe it off. It maybe explains why he keeps having different girlfriends and is never able to get one to marry him so that he can have a kid like me.

'It's just for a few days.'

'What is?' I said.

Uncle Bill sighed. 'She's not very well, Cym. Your mum.'

I remembered what she'd said to me yesterday. 'Has she still got her headache?'

'Sort of. So she's gone away,' Uncle Bill said.

'What?'

'She's gone away, Cym.'

'Because of a *headache*?'

'Sort of. Though . . .'

'She's in a hospital?'

'Yes. A . . . hospital.'

'For people with headaches, or other things too?'

'Mostly headaches. But it won't be for long. A few days. Just till she's better, okay, champ?'

I stared at Uncle Bill and then I jumped out of bed. I ran into Mum's room, not because I didn't believe him but because I had to see for myself. That she'd gone. She's my mum, after all. But he was right. Mum's room was empty. Not *empty* empty, as there were lots of things in it, but empty of her. So really, really empty, all of her stuff just standing there, almost looking embarrassed.

Her duvet was creased up and it reminded me of the dream I'd had. Brown water, all choppy and angry, twisting round upon itself. It made me swallow so I turned round and went back out to the landing.

Uncle Bill put his arm over my shoulder and interfered with my hair.

'Chin up,' he said.

Now, at this point, I'm wondering what you out there in Reading Land are thinking. Perhaps it is 'OUCH, the *poor kid*. It wasn't like he was overly blessed with parents to begin with and now he's down to NONE. That's four–nil to Lance (at least until Cym's mum gets better).' But maybe you're not. 'Hold on,' you might be thinking. 'This Uncle Bill chap is clearly a dude. He bought our Cymbeline a Scalextric set, don't forget. So maybe Cym is about to get some extra *stuff* from this Uncle Bill, to make up for the fact that his mum's gone totally zipwire.' Well, if you are thinking that, then in a small sense you are right. Uncle Bill led me downstairs and asked what I normally have for breakfast.

'KitKats.'

'*Really?*'

'On Tuesdays. They're my Tuesday breakfast.'

I'm not sure he believed me, but he let me have a couple anyway. Something must have happened to them, though, because they didn't taste very good. I didn't even finish the second one. Uncle Bill poured me a glass of milk and then looked up at the wall clock.

'Better get dressed.'

'What should I wear?'

He frowned. 'School uniform. Yesterday's will be fine, though you'll need to find some pants and socks.'

'Oh. We're not going to see her then? In hospital?'

Uncle Bill took a breath. 'Maybe later. I'm not sure. After school. Perhaps. I have to find out, Cym, okay?'

Okay?! That was the last word I was going to agree with. How could he possibly ask me if anything was *okay*? I didn't argue, though. I just shrugged and went to get dressed. When I was done we left the house and Uncle Bill turned to me.

'How do you normally get to school?'

'Taxi,' I said, though this time he wasn't buying it and he took me off to the bus stop.

It's weird. Yesterday, the worst, most terrible and embarrassing thing in the HISTORY OF THE WORLD had happened. But, as we got off the bus and walked across the heath to my school, it was nowhere. I wasn't thinking about it. I'd been pushed into a swimming pool. The entire class had seen me *without anything on*. And that wasn't everything. Oh no, it actually got much worse. We hadn't just gone back to school after the pool. Instead Miss Phillips had called my mum to come and get me. Mum cycled to the pool from Messy Art and went nuclear. Everyone stared in amazement as she screamed at Miss Phillips and the man in the red polo shirt for not looking after me properly. She glared at the kids, demanding to know who had pushed me in. Billy Lee went white as paper. I just stood there, aware that this would be news for weeks, months, even forever, a school legend that would be passed on from year to year until, eventually, my own children would run home from school and tell me all about THE NUDE KID WITH THE CRAZY MUM. But now I didn't care. There was a huge hollowness deep inside me that made everything else seem trivial. My.

Mum. Was. Gone. She'd never gone, not ever. It was her and me, always. I felt empty, sucked out, and when I saw Lance pushing his bike in through the school gates I realised something else. He'd asked me a simple question about swimming and I'd lied to him. I'd said I was really good. Because of that I'd ended up at the bottom of the swimming pool and because of *that*, my mum had somehow got ill. So ill she'd had to go to the hospital.

So it was *all my fault*.

Uncle Bill started to say goodbye but I shook my head.

'I'm not going in. I'm going to see my mum.'

'Cym . . .'

'I'm going to see my mum,' I said again. 'And nothing's going to stop me.'

At that, Uncle Bill sighed and he did this open-mouthed thinking thing. Then he made some calls, said 'thank you' a lot, and I knew he was talking to work. Uncle Bill is the head of a charity that looks after vulnareb . . . vulnorib . . . vulenerob . . . people who need help. He's like super busy doing that but he seemed to have sorted things out as he gave me a thumbs-up, before going into his phone again. This next conversation didn't go as well. He got a bit cross and, even though he turned away from me, I heard him say things like, 'We *both* have to help,' and, 'Last time, you didn't do a *thing*, did you?' But eventually he seemed to have sorted out whatever it was and he put his arm round my shoulder.

'Come on then,' he said. We walked up the little hill from school and I pretended not to see Veronique Chang getting out of her mum's Volvo.

'Cymbeline!' she called out.

'Cym?' Uncle Bill said, when I ignored Veronique. 'Aren't you going to . . .?'

'Not me,' I said. 'Different boy. There's a Cymbeline in Year Five.'

'Oh,' Uncle Bill said, and we walked off to the train station.

CHAPTER EIGHT

It didn't take long. Four stops from Blackheath to somewhere called Welling. *Good name for a place with a hospital*, I thought. We got off the train and walked down this long high street past a Cancer Research and a Mencap. Mum would probably have dragged me into both of them. We're always going in charity shops, for books and coats and stuff. Christmas cards in January, because she likes to be prepared. Last summer she bought this dress from the Oxfam in Blackheath Village. She loved it and was all smiley when she wore it, though on the heath after school one day Billy Lee's mum told her that *she* had one just like it.

'Well, I *used* to have,' she said. And then she did

this loud sniggering laugh, and Mum went red. She doesn't wear it any more.

After going past a Greggs that smelled of sausage rolls we turned into some side streets. Uncle Bill didn't need a map or anything and that made me frown.

'Have you been here before?'

Uncle Bill looked annoyed with himself. I don't think he meant to give that away.

'You have, haven't you?'

'Yes.'

'To see my mum?' He nodded. 'Has she been in this hospital before?' He nodded again and I nodded back. It probably happened in that weird time Mum sometimes speaks about: BEFORE YOU WERE BORN. An odd time that, interesting in a way, though not particularly relevant to anything. 'Before I was . . .?'

'No, Cym. When you were a baby.'

'And Mum went into *hospital*? Who looked after me?'

'I did.'

'Oh,' I said, and my insides felt strange. It was shaky to hear that Mum had been in hospital before, but knowing Uncle Bill had looked after me made me feel shy, and warm inside. I put my hand in his and he squeezed it.

'Did I visit her?'

'I took you every day.'

'So was she in there for quite a while? How long's she going to be in this time?' I had a terrible thought. 'She WILL be out for my birthday, won't she?'

Uncle Bill looked caught out again and, suddenly, very serious. But he answered with nothing more than a shrug, and led me down some more side streets until we were walking towards the gates of a soggy-looking park.

'Wait,' I said, before we got there.

There was a greengrocer's outside the park with fruit all piled up. There were flowers too, in a bucket. I led Uncle Bill towards it and picked some – red ones, Mum's favourite colour. Uncle Bill handed them to the lady and she put paper round them. Bill gave her a fiver, which I said I'd give him back from my money box, and he gave them to me to hold. We walked into the park and I saw some swings and a duck pond, and an old-looking building over on the far side. When Uncle Bill looked at it I knew that was where we were going and I had a picture of Mum in her bed, with lots of other ladies in a row. She'd have her favourite nightie on and a bandage round her head for the headache. Mum would sit up, beaming, when she saw me. We'd put the flowers in a vase. The first thing she'd say was of course she'd be out by Saturday. I'd get my spellings out and we'd go through them like we always did on Tuesday mornings and Mum would try not to giggle at some of the answers I gave. She'd tell the other ladies I was her little champion. She'd kiss me and I'd say, 'Get well soon,' and then I'd be really careful not to hurt her head when I hugged her goodbye. She'd wave at me through the window when we left – her *special* boy.

The picture cheered me up and I told myself off. This wouldn't be so bad. Mums went into hospital all the time. Lance's did last year. His new-dad came to get him from school and when he came back next day his mum had had a baby.

'So you've got a sister?'

'A half-sister.'

'Which half is your sister?'

'The top,' he said. 'Definitely.'

I started to glow inside at the thought of seeing Mum and I pulled Bill to go faster. We got to the building, which was made out of dark red bricks that were black round the edges. We stood in front of a heavy blue door until a buzzer sounded and the door clicked open. We walked into a really bright reception and up to a big desk with two nurses behind it, one of them typing on a computer. The other left us standing there for a few minutes as she wrote something. Then, without looking up, she asked how she could help.

'We're here to see Janet Igloo,' Bill said and I wished he'd just said 'Mum'. I didn't like hearing her name like that.

The nurse picked up a phone, asking us to take a seat and wait, pressing it against her chest until we'd turned away. We moved to the other side of the room and sat down at a low table with magazines on. I picked one up that had Prince William and Princess Kate on the front. They were holding their baby. Prince William was smiling and I stared into his face for a bit, before putting the magazine down.

'Mr Martin?' the doctor said.

He'd come out of a side door that clicked shut behind him. A very tall, thin man with a goatee beard and round glasses. I only realised who *Mr Martin* was when Uncle Bill stood up.

'You're Ms Igloo's next of kin?' His voice was really

deep, almost like he was about to sing.

'Yes,' Bill said. 'Her brother.'

'I remember. Well, I'm Dr Mara, if you recall. And this handsome young man must be . . .?'

'Cymbeline,' Uncle Bill said. The doctor smiled at me and then asked if he could have a *quiet word* with Uncle Bill. He led him off towards the desk where the nurses were and I watched as they spoke. I was desperate to see Mum and wondered if she knew I was coming, trying to picture her face when she saw me. When Uncle Bill called me over I was about to ask him, but the look on his face stopped me. I turned to the doctor, who interfered with my hair.

'Is Mum's head better?'

'It isn't,' the doctor said. 'Not yet. And because of that –'

'We'll leave her alone today,' said Uncle Bill, doing cheerful badly again, like he had that morning. 'Let her get some rest.'

I stared at him. 'But we brought her some flowers.'

'I know. The nurses can give them to her. Okay?'

That word again. IT WAS NOT OKAY. I turned from him to the doctor.

'Have you got a toilet?' I said.

The doctor smiled and nodded, looking at the nurses, expecting them to help me. But they were both busy. I winced and squeezed my legs together and the doctor looked a little panicky. When I started to jump up and down he waved me to follow him towards the door he'd come out of, typing in some numbers on a keypad. He held the door for me and I went through it, into a narrow corridor with yellow walls. I waved back through the door at Uncle Bill, and the doctor showed me a green button to press when I wanted to come back out again. He walked towards a toilet door and I thanked him, just as a little device on his belt went beep. He looked at it, stopped, then hurried off up the corridor as I pushed the toilet door open.

But I didn't go inside.

The doctor turned a corner and the corridor was empty. I started up it, ready to duck to the side if he came back. My heart was pounding and I realised something. Actually being in there made me realise it. My image of what would happen inside here was only that – an image. I'd made it up. What if I found something else? Something worse. I stared at the corner the doctor had turned down and wondered if I should go back. I even turned, before telling myself that I had to go forward, and I did that and . . .

'Wow!' I said out loud.

In front of me was the least hospitally-looking hospital I'd ever seen. To start with there were no people on plastic chairs complaining about how long they'd been waiting and staring up at a display in case they missed their names. Instead I was in a big space, with sofas, chairs and a carpet, and big pictures on the walls. The colours were not like hospitals normally are, all greys and browns. Instead they were soft and bright, like Starburst flavours. I was instantly cheered up, more so when I walked past people who were just sitting, reading or chatting, drinking tea, none looking particularly injured or anything. One had a name thingy round her neck that told me she was a nurse, though she wasn't dressed like one and she wasn't injecting anyone or taking their temperature. She was just *talking*.

It was such a relief. Mum wouldn't mind staying in a place like this, would she? I looked around, hoping to spot her. I was about to ask the nurse where she was after I'd seen Mum wasn't there. But I didn't, because I'd heard something. It came from the other side of the space, making me smile, and I hurried towards it, stopping at an open door. I peered in. This room was smaller, though just as nice as the big space, and I was sure Mum would be in there because she LOVES *The Simpsons*. When I ask for a biscuit after school she says 'okely dokely'. When she forgets the house keys she says 'doh', like Homer. If *The Simpsons* was on she was bound to be watching it. Only she wasn't. No one was. I blinked, wondering why you'd have a room with a TV on, with no one in it, though it didn't matter. Mum would explain it to me. I backed out and went on, past more rooms, looking into the ones with doors open. The first was a little kitchen and the next had a chair like a dentist's, with machines all around it. I was wondering if I'd ever find Mum, when I came to another door, this one at the end of a corridor.

This room was more like the place I'd been picturing. To start with it did have beds in. They were bigger than I'd imagined, though, and further apart – two completely surrounded by curtains. The rest did have ladies in but none of them had a bandage on. One was an old woman staring up at the ceiling. Next to her was a woman in a duffel coat and seeing her stopped me. She was sitting up and it looked like she was washing her hands. She didn't have a sink, but she was still doing that. My throat went dry and I wanted to back out, hoping she wouldn't see me, knowing that I must be in the wrong room. But when I looked over at the next bed, there she was. Mum. Like the woman next to her, Mum was sitting on her bed. Not in her favourite nightie. Dressed. She didn't have a bandage on her head either and I thought that might mean she was better now. I was so happy to see her. Just to see her of course, but also to say sorry – for lying to Lance about swimming. I was about to run forward but I found myself hesitating. Mum has a thing about her hair. She washes it *all the time*, but now it was tangly. She looked, in fact, like she'd been 'dragged through a hedge backwards' and she wasn't sitting up straight either, like she was always telling me, but squashed over forward, fiddling with something in her hand.

'Mum? *The Simpsons* are on.'

She didn't hear. She just carried on staring at the thing in her hand, which she was pressing against her stomach. Then I realised that she was speaking, her voice really quiet, though I could just hear what she was saying.

'*Two sugars*,' she said. '*Two. Sugars.*'

What?

She said it over and over, and I didn't understand. There was no one to say it to, for one thing; she was just speaking into space. And she doesn't even *take* sugar. I was about to ask what she meant but then I saw what she was holding.

Mr Fluffy.

Mum was pressing him against her tummy. So *that's* why he wasn't in my bed that morning. I stared as she twisted his left eye and I wanted to tell her to be careful in case she pulled it off. But I didn't, because, all of a sudden, I was afraid. Of my mum. I didn't like that about myself and I asked myself how it could be. I couldn't help it, though, and when I tried to walk forward I couldn't move. I just watched as Mum crushed Mr Fluffy to her face and began to sob, rooting me to the spot until a hand landed on my shoulder.

'Come on, Cym,' said Uncle Bill.

CHAPTER NINE

I didn't go in to see Mum. Instead I let Uncle Bill lead me back past all the charity shops and the Greggs.

'Oh no,' I said, as we walked up on to the platform.

'What is it, Cym?'

I didn't answer. I just held up the flowers I'd bought for Mum, and which I was still holding in my hand.

I don't remember much of what happened for the rest of that day. After Uncle Bill took me back to school I had to wait a bit before going in. Mum's crying, I must have inherited it. When it stopped I was still in a daze, like being at the bottom of that swimming pool. Then I was just confused, picturing Mum with Mr Fluffy. She never lets me take him out of the house any more in case he goes missing.

So why on earth did she take him with her?

Uncle Bill hadn't thought about giving me any lunch and, by the time I'd got into the hall, the Year 4 sitting was over. Mrs Stebbings offered to make me a sandwich but I wasn't hungry. She said to run out on to the heath with my friends but that was the last thing I wanted to do. I went round to my classroom instead and got one of the spelling test sheets from Miss Phillips's desk because I'd missed it that morning. I remembered what the words were as best I could before putting the sheet on the pile with the others. Veronique's was on the top, her words are harder than the ones for the rest of us (she even has lessons on her own sometimes). The first one Miss Phillips had given her to spell was 'precocious'. The second was 'presumptuous'. Then 'conceited', 'arrogant', 'haughty', 'immodest', 'complacent' and 'supercilious'. I don't know if she got them right or not.

I didn't go out at playtime. When everyone came back in I didn't look at anyone; I just got out my book for private reading. At home time I was expecting to see Uncle Bill out in the playground, but he wasn't there. Instead it was Auntie Mill who was waiting for me.

Auntie Mill had her hands on her hips and was holding her car keys, tapping her foot as she stared around at all the kids. She didn't see me until I was right in front of her.

'Oh,' she said. 'There you are. So how are . . .? I mean, come along then. Have you got everything?'

I held my bag up, and Mum's flowers. Auntie Mill frowned at them for a second before taking them. 'Oh, how . . . sweet,' she said. 'Thank you, Cymbeline.'

'Oh, no, they're not for . . .'

I couldn't finish what I was going to say because Auntie Mill had turned towards the gates with the flowers in her hand. Ignoring Marcus Breen doing a drowning mime, I jogged behind her, out of the playground to where Auntie Mill had broken Rule 4 of the St Saviour's school code. She'd driven right down to the gates instead of parking at the top of the road, thereby *putting the lives of St Saviour's children at risk*. I looked for Reception kids squashed on to the tyres but fortunately there weren't any. The car bleeped and flashed and I tried to pull the door open without success.

'Need to grow a bit,' Auntie Mill said, yanking it open for me.

Now, what I'm going to say next is controversial. Sometimes our parents have *opinions* and while they *always* assume that we'll *share* those opinions (because we're their children) sometimes we DO NOT. My mum, for instance, says that a band called Abba are great, but that is COMPLETELY NOT TRUE. What she also says is that Auntie Mill's car is 'tacky' and 'hideous', a 'gas-guzzling planet killer', the sort of car driven by people with 'frail egos' and 'no social conscience'. She doesn't say this to Auntie Mill but to Uncle Bill, and, while I never comment, I disagree. Any car would be great as we don't have one, but Auntie Mill's car is EPIC. It is E-NORMOUS. It is black and shiny (which you know I like) and so high off the ground you could do with a rope ladder to get yourself in. The windows are tinted so you can do faces at people while you drive along and it has these leather seats that warm your bum up (a bit surprising the first time, I can tell you). The front seats have actually got *TVs on the back*. My cousins Juniper and Clayton have their own stashes of sweets in handy pouch things, and they don't even have to ask Auntie Mill if they can eat them – they just do! I love Auntie Mill's car almost as much as she does. On the rare times she comes round, she keeps looking out on to our street to make sure it's still there.

'Where are Juni and Clay?' I said, as the car lurched forward. I was in the front seat on a booster. The road was full of people walking up to the heath and Auntie Mill pressed the horn, making them jump and turn round. She tutted and sighed, edging through when they walked over to the pavement.

'Fencing,' she said. 'Well, Juni*per* is. I normally watch, though today –'

'And Clay?'

'Clay*ton* is at debating club.'

'Are we going to pick them up?'

'That's right.'

'And are they coming to stay at our house too?'

Auntie Mill slowed down a bit to look horrified. '*Your* house?'

'Until Mum's better.'

'Oh,' she said, going on again and pushing in front of Rachel's mum's Mini. 'No, Cymbeline, we won't be going back to your house. You'll be . . .'

'Yes?'

Auntie Mill sighed. 'Staying with us. And Uncle Bill. We'll be . . . sharing you. Until your mum gets better.'

'Oh. Do *you* know when that might be?'

'No,' she said. 'I'm sorry to say that I don't, Cymbeline.'

Auntie Mill pulled into the traffic as I sat watching the St Saviour's kids coming out on to the heath. I tried to take in what Auntie Mill had said, and I tried to be positive about it. Their house is BIG. The garden is like a park, with a treehouse and bushes to hide in, some proper goalposts and swings at the bottom. It has also suffered, in Mum's phrase, a 'digital apocalypse', by which she means that Clay and Juni both have iPads and that Clay's got an Xbox, and Juni's got a PS4 IN HER BEDROOM. I overheard Uncle Bill offering to buy me an Xbox last Christmas but Mum said NO WAY!

'Why not?' I wailed, when he'd gone home.

'Because I'd quite like my son to remain a human being.'

'But Clay's a human being, isn't he?'

'How would I know?' Mum had said. 'For the last four years I've only ever seen the back of his head.'

I should, therefore, have been happy at the idea of going to Auntie Mill's. But I *wanted* to be at home. Being there would feel closer to Mum. Her *things* would be there and there would be photos I could look at.

'But I don't have any stuff,' I said.

'Clayton's got some old clothes. Pants and things.'

'What about school uniform?'

'You can wear what you have. And if it gets dirty Clayton's got some. I don't think a school like yours would bother too much if you came in wearing a different jumper, would they?'

'I don't know. But . . .?'

'What, Cymbeline?'

I pretended to be embarrassed. 'How will I get to sleep?'

'*To sleep?*'

'Without Mr Fluffy,' I said, like I was confessing to something.

At that, Auntie Mill sighed, and put the brakes on. I could see her deciding, and then I could see *what* she'd decided. Clearly, she did not want me to be unable to get to sleep while staying with her, so instead of going up through Blackheath Village to their house she turned right across the little roundabout at the last moment, getting a beep from Danny Jones's dad. She ignored that and sped up, and pretty soon we were parked outside our house.

'I'll wait here,' she said, as I pushed the door open. 'Don't be long, please.'

I jumped down to the pavement and looked at our front door. A free newspaper was sticking out of the letterbox and I poked it under my arm. I dug around in my bag for the spare keys, which Mum keeps in there because she's always locking herself out. I'm an artist, she tells me, which apparently explains it.

I opened the house and stepped into the hall. It felt odd, and a little scary, to be in there on my own. I stepped forward, the floorboards squeaking beneath my feet. I went into the kitchen and put the paper on to the table next to mine and Uncle Bill's breakfast things, which he hadn't cleared away. I did that, piling them up in the sink and getting a cloth for the crumbs. Then I climbed the stairs and stared at Mum's door for a bit before going in. I made her bed and then went into my room where I stuffed my *own* pants, and my *own* socks, and my *own* pyjamas into my bag, as well as some school clothes. Auntie Mill was wrong. If we even wore blue socks instead of grey ones, Miss Phillips made us stay in at lunch. And what did she mean when she said 'a school like yours'? Was it different from Juni and Clay's school in some way?

I put some Asterix books in and then went down to the living room where I had a decision to make. But Mum wouldn't mind – not if she knew why I wanted it. I slid it in with the books and clothes and ran upstairs again and grabbed a random teddy from the shelf above my bed.

'Mr Fluffy,' I told Auntie Mill, holding it up as I climbed back into the car. It was a fib of course, because it wasn't really Mr Fluffy. I would like to apologise for that. At least I had my own stuff, though.

Some boys from the estate came round the corner and pointed at us, clearly admiring Auntie Mill's car as much as I did. Auntie Mill saw them and shoved her foot down, the tyres squealing as we shot away. Show off! She drove us to fencing, which was at Juni and Clay's school, and when we got there I could sort of understand what she meant by 'a school like yours'. Because their school certainly *was* different. The car park was three times bigger than our playground and the sports hall she led me into was enormous. It was also just a sports hall. Unlike ours, it wasn't a dining hall as well. I trod on a squashed chip once playing murder ball in PE and I nearly broke my neck.

When we walked in I gawped at all the space the

kids had and then stared at some photos on the wall. They showed, it said, the Langham School Year 4 Journey. Our school journeys are to Camber Sands. Last year it was drizzling, which was a relief because the year before that it had bucketed it down. A bit of a contrast to what I was looking at because these kids had been to Spain!

Now this made me pretty jealous I can tell you, and I wondered how one school could be one way, and another school a different way completely. Weren't we all just, well, *kids*? What I wasn't expecting to be envious of, however, was Juniper's fencing. This, I imagined, was some sort of craft activity involving PVA glue, staples and bamboo. What it was, I soon realised, was not fencing at all. It was sword fighting! Lots of kids in padded white clothes and black mesh masks were trying to hit each other with *real metal swords*! It looked BRILLIANT. I sat down on a low bench with Auntie Mill and just stared, TOTALLY JEALOUS now, though the idea of Marcus Breen with a sword in his hand was terrifying no matter how much protection you had on.

I sent my eyes around all the kids, trying to pick out Juni. With everyone wearing masks I couldn't see her, though Auntie Mill must have read my thoughts because she pointed towards the wall.

'That's her,' she said, sitting up. I wondered how she knew until I saw the initials on the back of her suit: JW (Juniper Winters).

Juni was standing opposite someone a little shorter than her. She wasn't fighting but waiting while a man attached a long wire to her belt. Auntie Mill explained that it was for scoring. A beep sounded if you hit your opponent or if you got hit yourself.

'She's having a proper match then?'

'She's training for a tournament. She's really very talented, Cymbeline. You should be proud of her.'

I said I was, and it was true. A sword fighting tournament?! The other kid got wired up and the fight began. In the sword fights I have with Lance we slash at each other, jump off the sofa and shout out that we are either Luke Skywalker or Darth Vader. Juniper and the other kid didn't shout or jump, however, and they didn't slash each other. At first they didn't do anything, just faced each other before Juniper took a step forward. The other kid stepped back. Then the kid stepped forward and Juniper stepped back. They did this quite a few more times and I began to get bored. But then Juniper really went for it. In a flash she leapt forward, lunging with her sword, the other kid knocking it away until the two blades were clashing together in a crazy-mad flurry. BRILLIANT! A beep sounded and I leapt up to my feet.

'Yes!'

'*No*, Cymbeline,' Auntie Mill said, grabbing my arm and pulling me down. 'That was *against* Juniper.'

'Oh.'

'A lucky counter-riposte. It happens.'

It certainly did. I watched again. Again Juniper and the other kid did this dance thing before Juniper got brave and leapt forward. There was whirling and a beep and I was sure that Juniper had won until Auntie Mill sort of hissed, which told me that the other kid had got that point too. Another lucky counter-riposte, I whispered to Auntie Mill, though after the fifth time I said it she told me to be quiet. When it happened for the seventh time in a row (how unlucky can you get?!) the other kid stepped forward and thrust out the hand that wasn't holding the sword. I thought Juniper was going to shake it but instead she did something AWESOME.

She pulled her mask off and bunged it at the wall! And then she threw her sword off after it!

WOW!

Was this part of fencing? Is this what you have to do if you are the victim of seven lucky counter-ripostes? I wanted to ask Auntie Mill but she was rushing over to Juni, who didn't seem very happy.

'I hate this stupid sport!' she screamed, before marching off towards the exit with Auntie Mill behind her.

Blimey.

I wanted to cheer Juni up. I wanted to tell her that she was very talented, and that *lucky counter-ripostes happen.* I'm proud of you, I wanted to say, but instead I was aware of something odd. Very odd. For the other kid had turned from Juniper and was facing . . . me.

And then he was walking over.

I swallowed, staring into the black mesh of the helmet as it bore down on me. I pushed myself to my feet, backing up against the wall with the Year 4 Spanish journey on, staring at the sword in the kid's hand. If your opponent flounces off, are you allowed to kill their relatives? I swallowed, and then swallowed again when I heard something very bizarre.

My name.

'Cymbeline!'

The kid stopped and instead of running me through he took his helmet off.

He? No, not he.

Veronique Chang was staring at me.

Again.

CHAPTER TEN

When Auntie Mill had told me that I was going back to her house I'd been disappointed but at least, I'd thought, it would be a humiliation-free zone. Juni and Clay aren't at my school so they wouldn't know what had happened at the swimming pool, would they? This dream vanished when Veronique and Juni came out of the changing rooms together . . .

AND WALKED OVER TO AUNTIE MILL'S CAR.

'I live next door,' Veronique explained.

'Yes,' Auntie Mill said, yanking open her door. '*We* introduced Veronique to fencing and the school coach said she could come as a special favour *to us*. And now, Veronique, you have the . . . You seem to be coming along . . . well.'

'She's good at lucky counter-ripostes.'

'It's very mathematical,' Veronique said, climbing into the back after me. 'Which I like.' Juni didn't say anything. She just snatched at her seatbelt before glaring out of the window. But when I scooted in next to her she seemed, finally, to notice me.

'What's Cymbeline doing here? Is he going to start fencing too?'

'Wow,' I said, leaning forward between the seats. 'That would be epic, Auntie Mill. If you could ask as a special favour, then I could –'

'I don't think so,' Auntie Mill replied. 'One favour is probably enough. And the kit is expensive so I don't think your mum could . . . Anyway, Auntie Janet isn't well, Juniper.'

'Has she gone wacko again?'

'Juniper! That's not a phrase you should use.'

'*You* did, on the phone this morning to Uncle Bill. Is that what you were arguing about?'

'I was *not* arguing. I was discussing what would be best for Cymbeline. Auntie Janet is a little unwell and so Cymbeline will be at our house tonight.'

'Well, he's not sleeping in my room,' Juni said.

With that, Juni hit some buttons on the TV in

front of her and a programme about kids with alien parents came on. I was going to watch but Juni pulled some headphones out of one of the handy pockets and shoved them over her ears so I couldn't hear. This left me alone with Veronique and I winced, hoping that Clay would come out of debating club soon so that I could talk to him.

But Auntie Mill got a text and told us that Clay*ton* was getting a lift home with some other parents. She pulled out of the car park and I swallowed, really nervous about sitting next to Veronique. She still smelled like someone somewhere was eating candyfloss and I couldn't understand because she'd been really sweaty when she took her mask off. The last time Lance came round we played football in the ball court up the road and afterwards he smelled like someone somewhere had *died*. Being next to her was excruciating, though. She'd seen me humiliated, first in the swimming pool and then when my mum came. Forget the Weetabix, how could she like me now?

I watched the alien parents with the sound off until we got to Auntie Mill's house. We all piled out into the driveway and I waited for Juni and Veronique to run in together and talk about what happened in the pool. But – phew – it didn't happen. Juni stomped over to the front door while Veronique stood there with her fencing bag in her hand.

'Thank you for driving me home, Mrs Winters.'

'Well, that's okay, Veronique.'

'Until next week then.'

'Yes. Okay. I suppose.'

Auntie Mill turned to the house and I followed, before Veronique could say anything to me.

For tea (which they call supper) Auntie Mill gave us pizza, and even though I'd had it yesterday I didn't say anything. Nor did I say that Auntie Mill's pizza (from Marks & Spencer) was nowhere near as good as Mum's pizza (from Iceland). Mum's pizza (from Iceland) is flat, and doesn't have anything on to ruin the taste, while Auntie Mill's pizza (from Marks & Spencer) was too big and had this thing called *artichoke* on, which I hope never to see again. I didn't say anything, though. I ate the edges like I'd eaten the middle the day before and then I ate some carrot sticks. Auntie Mill gave us bowls of cut-up orange, apples, bananas and grapes after, all mixed in together. There wasn't any pudding.

'Right,' Auntie Mill said, tipping sugar into a cup of coffee. 'What do you two feel like doing?'

I wanted to play on Juni's PS4 and she wanted to do the same. Apparently, though, she felt very strongly about doing this *on her own*. Auntie Mill took her off for a 'chat' about this and, while I was waiting at the table, Clay came in, though at first I didn't recognise him. As I said, we don't see Auntie Mill and her family much and it had been ages since last time. Clay was now big, with long hair. And he was ill, some disease attacking his face. He had this red rash on and there were little straggly hairs above his mouth. My mum gets these but she pulls them out with tweezers. I made a note to mention tweezers to Clay but in the meantime asked if he wanted a game of football.

'Sorry,' he said, stuffing a slice of my pizza into his mouth. 'Homework.' When Auntie Mill and Juni came back in he said, ''Right, Mum. Dad home?'

'No. He had to go to Zurich. A crisis came up this morning. Just after I spoke to your Uncle Bill, oddly enough.'

'Right. But before you ask, Cymbeline's not sleeping in my room, okay?'

Auntie Mill shook her head and went off to sort

out the 'sleeping arrangements', and the other two disappeared. I wandered out into the garden and played football on my own, beating me and Lance's kick-up record, though Lance would have said it didn't count as the ball was flat. Clay can't have used it for a while and he can't have used the goalposts either because they'd fallen over and were covered in wet leaves. I walked over to the swing but the seat was hanging off so I climbed into the treehouse instead. Last summer I played Cowboys and Native Americans in there with Juni and Clay. Or was it the summer before? It was great but as I sat on the mouldy floor I knew we'd never play it again. Juni was only a year older than me but now, suddenly, she felt much older than that. And Clay felt like a different species. It was like the Juni and Clay I had known had disappeared and I wondered: is that what growing up is? Disappearing, and reappearing as someone else? I wished Lance was there because he'd think the treehouse was boomtastic. Would Auntie Mill let me ask him round?

I was climbing back down from the treehouse when I stopped. The plastic box! It was still there, underneath the little table. Juni and I had filled it with sweets and then defended it against Clay. I climbed back in to see if the sweets were still there, but they weren't. The box had half a packet of Auntie Mill's cigarettes inside, some of the filling spilling out. You're not allowed to smoke with kids around any more so she must have to come here to do it. At least someone was using the treehouse.

Halfway down the ladder I stopped because I thought I heard Juni calling my name. But it wasn't her. Veronique was waving at me from her bathroom window. I pretended not to see, running back into the house instead where Auntie Mill was lying on the sofa.

'Want to sit down?' she asked, looking up from the telly. '*Someone* round here might want to spend some time with me.'

I thought about it but when I looked at the screen I saw that it was that thing about cakes. I'm all for cakes, don't get me wrong, but watching a telly programme about making them? *Toc! Toc! These grown-ups are crazy.*

'Thanks,' I said. 'But can I go to bed?'

Auntie Mill shrugged and swung her legs off the sofa, setting a big glass of lemonade down on the coffee table. She led me past Clay's room and then Juni's, which used to have My Little Pony stickers on the door, though these had been peeled off. They looked like My Little Pony ghosts. I was going to sleep in the guest room, which we normally weren't even allowed to play in. My schoolbag was on the bed.

'Do you need pyjamas?'

'I brought my own.'

'Good. You'll need to be up at seven tomorrow, but not before then, *please.* There's a clock on the bedside table, though – sorry, can you tell the time?'

Tell the time! Of course I could. It was like she really didn't know me at all. I said yes and put my pyjamas on. I cleaned my teeth with a new brush Auntie Mill gave me and then she walked me back to the spare room.

'Have you got your . . .?'

'Mr Fluffy?'

I pulled out the random teddy from my bag, and climbed on to the huge bed, moving up so Auntie Mill could give me a cuddle. But she turned her head out of the doorway. There was cheering from the TV. It was the cakes. Auntie Mill said a quick goodnight and then hurried off down the stairs.

When she was gone I stared at the back of the shut door. And took a breath. For it was only then – without

Juni or Clay or Auntie Mill or the *real* Mr Fluffy – that I properly got a sense of my situation. I'd be staying there. Auntie Mill had told me that Uncle Bill had gone away for work – for a whole WEEK. So I'd be there on my own. I looked around: the room was so tidy it was like no one had ever been in it. The carpet was soft and white and there were shiny turquoise curtains. A painting on the wall showed old-fashioned grown-ups dancing on a beach. It was all very nice, but it smelled funny, sort of like flowers made out of metal. And the bed was too big. How long would I be staying there? I felt like Oliver, all alone. It was a good job I didn't like the artichoke pizza so I didn't have to ask for any MORE.

Cymbeline! William! Igloo! I sat up and told myself off. I didn't need to feel like this. Not after going home earlier. I reached into my bag and pushed aside the Asterix books until I found the thing that I'd really got Auntie Mill to take me home for.

Mum's tablet.

The tablet was in its case and I slid it out. I typed in Mum's super-secret password (Springfield) and then found her photos file. We'd only made it on Sunday, loading up pictures from our camera and Mum's phone. I went into it and found what I was looking for.

Mum.

There were pictures of her. Lots of little ones, and all I had to do was touch one to wake her up. And there she'd be. Right in front of me, right there in the room.

I found myself smiling. I wasn't alone. I touched the first one and stared at it. I'd taken it on Christmas Day. Mum was wearing a paper hat and smiling so wide it was like her smile was her whole face. I smiled too and swiped into the next: Mum in our garden on Bonfire Night, orange lines in front of her face from the sparklers. I found more, and it was so good to see her. She was smiling in all of them, even the one taken on Sunday at the National Gallery by the little girl who'd grabbed my leg. She didn't quite have the top of her head, but her smile was still there. This was my mum – not that woman in the hospital – and she was going to be out soon anyway. The weekend was ages away. I nodded to myself and then stared, as I realised something else. Some of the little pictures had video cameras next to them, so I didn't need to be jealous of Harry Potter, did I? I had moving photos too! Okay, the first six were of me trying to beat my kick-up record but I soon found one of Mum from last summer. We were in our tent.

'*No*,' she groaned from inside her sleeping bag. 'It's too early. *Go. Back. To. Sleep.*'

The next one was a double movie selfie, both of us jumping up and down at Charlton after Johnnie Jackson got the winner. I watched that one five times and then just lay there, thinking about Mum and wondering if she was thinking about me too.

CHAPTER ELEVEN

'*Line up, everyone. Chop-chop, hurry along now.*'

That was Miss Phillips. The next day. But don't worry, we weren't going back to the swimming pool. Today was a school trip. I'd forgotten about it and didn't ask Auntie Mill to make me any sandwiches. Mrs Stebbings made me some instead, before interfering with my hair. I thanked her and ran round into the corridor where a boy I thought was Lance was hanging his cycle hat on his peg.

'Lance,' I said (because I thought it was him).

The boy I thought was Lance did not answer.

'*Lance*,' I said again.

The boy I thought was Lance still did not answer and I looked at him. He had Lance's bag, with the

Charlton team written on in Sharpie ('Jackson' all the way down to 'Igloo'). He had Lance's coat. He also had Lance's face, which really should have proved that it was him. But the boy said, 'I'm not Lance.'

This made me frown, and I looked at the boy I thought was Lance until I was sure, like you are with a sum you're checking. It. Was. Lance.

'Yes you are,' I said.

'No I'm not.'

'Yes you *are*.'

'I'm *not*! I'm . . .'

'What?'

The boy I thought was Lance paused. 'I'm not Lance any more.'

'Why *not*?'

'Because I'm being called by my middle name now.'

'I didn't even know you had a middle name.'

'Well, I do. And my dad said I could use it.'

'Your . . .?'

'My *real* dad, right?'

'Right. But . . . what's wrong with Lance?'

'Nothing.'

'There must be, or you'd still be called it.'

The boy I thought was Lance sighed. 'Well. Even

though I'm not named after Lance Arm . . . and it's just a random name . . . my dad's started making jokes.'

'Your . . .?'

'My *new*-dad.'

'What kind of jokes?'

'I wanted to go out on my bike but he said I had to wee in a bottle first.'

'Why?'

'To test if I was on drugs.'

'Sounds like *he's* on drugs.'

'My real dad says that too. But I'm not Lance any more, understand?'

'I don't mind what you're called. But I think it's probably best if I know what that is.'

'Do you?'

'Yes.'

'Well, hard luck because I'm not telling you.'

'You're *not*? Why?'

'Because, Cymbeline Igloo, *that* would be talking to you. And I'm not talking to you ever AGAIN.'

And with that the boy I'd thought was Lance – and who really was Lance (but wasn't Lance) – stormed off into our classroom.

I stared, amazed, like someone in an old-fashioned

cartoon who gets hit in the face with a frying pan. I wondered what I'd done and I went after Not-Lance to ask, but I didn't get a chance. Instead I ran straight into Billy Lee and I stiffened, waiting for him to jeer, for this to be the beginning of all the *really funny* jokes about the swimming pool. But, instead of laughing, he shrank away, almost as if he was scared of me. I stared into his face as he swallowed and I noticed that he had a black eye. But I didn't give it to him, did I? I was about to ask him how he *did* get it when Miss Phillips told us all to get ready. And, for the first time ever, Billy was the first in line.

We were going to the Tate Modern art gallery and you don't have to worry about me this time because (unlike the swimming pool) I was used to this. Mum takes me to galleries all the time and Tate Modern is my favourite, largely because the pictures aren't all of old people (not like some galleries I could mention). There's also this slope you can do Heelying on. Even at the National, where Mum works, I get told off for doing that.

We got the train from Blackheath station to London Bridge. We walked from there and when we got to the Tate we put our bags in a room downstairs. Then we went upstairs, everyone looking around at the massive ceilings. I was next to Elizabeth Fisher but when we got to the top of the stairs I walked over to The Friend Formerly Known As Lance. I wanted to talk to him because, on the way there, I'd worked out why he was angry and it had got me really upset. We were *supposed* to be friends. We were in nursery together, and we'd had four joint birthday parties. He was the one I was supposed to be taking on my birthday outing this year. He's the only person I've ever had a sleepover with without my mum staying and I have *never once* been on the opposite side to him in lunchtime football.

And in spite of this, I lied to him. I told him I was epic at swimming. I wanted to tell him sorry, that it was just a *stupid thing to say*, that I only said it because I was nervous. But I couldn't because when he saw me coming he turned his head away and walked off. Then Miss Phillips put us in different groups and I sighed, hoping I could talk to him at lunchtime.

I went off with my group and the first thing we did was make nametags so the helpers would know what to call us. A helper then gave us each a big pad of paper and each group was given a different area of the gallery to explore. In my group was Elizabeth Fisher,

Danny Jones, Vi Delap and Vi Delap's mum. We had to find pictures to copy, something Danny said was weird, because why draw a picture that's already *been* drawn? But, once again, I was used to it, because Mum gets me to do the same thing, something that takes ages at places like the National or the Royal Academy. Another reason I like the Tate, though, is that in there it takes no time at all. Line-scribble-swish-dab: done. You can really see why artists don't bother painting old people any more and, if I'm an artist one day, I am *so* going to be a modern one.

We found some paintings by a man called Jackson Pollock. Vi's mum said they were famous. This was confusing because Marcus Breen did some just like them in class last year – all random swirls – and got really told off. I enjoyed doing copies, though. I started with green, going round and round, then doing the same thing with yellow, and red. Blue. And it was strange. I had so many difficult things making me think about them – Mum, 'Lance', swimming – but for the first time since the Charlton match it all disappeared. I was just there, trying to make the colours even, a feeling growing that I couldn't really understand. When I'm drawing a train, say, or a castle, I'm painting *that*, trying to make it look the same. But because *this* was just colours, and wasn't of anything *real*, it began to feel like I was drawing what was inside me. Trying to make everything line up and not be so sort of *jangly*. I got completely stuck in until Vi's mum looked over my shoulder.

'Wow,' she said. 'That's brilliant.'

I couldn't help smiling and then again when (after I'd finished) she took the picture to show Miss Phillips. Miss Phillips told her, yes, I was really talented, *just like my mum*. I smiled even more, and not just because she liked my picture. I never thought of myself as good at things. Veronique was, and David Finch. Billy (grrrr). But compared to the other pictures, which Miss Phillips put on a table, mine was good. I stared at them, some copies of a Picasso, others of Matisses, and others of paintings by someone called De Chirico, who always painted pictures with these long shadows on, though no one had got them all going the right way, quite.

It was even stranger because I hadn't *meant* mine to be good. It just came out that way, like someone else had done it from inside me. And that person had to be my mum because if I was good at art it was because I was *her son*. This thought made me even happier, a glow coming on inside me. And when I looked at my picture again, it grew even warmer. The colours *had* come together. They looked even, and calm. And this would happen with the difficult things inside me because if I'd made it happen in the picture I could make it happen in real life, couldn't I?

Starting with Lance.

I mean Not-Lance.

Not-Lance still wasn't talking to me. I thought I'd find him at lunch but the room they took us to had these long tables and he waited to see where I sat before going right off to the other end. Mrs Stebbings had given me two Penguins to cheer me up, which normally would have worked because they're my favourite, in spite of the fact that they're not actually shaped like penguins, which they should be. Mars bars too – they should be round. And red.

Anyway, I was going to give him one of the Penguins because his mum only ever lets him have yoghurts on school trips (which my mum says is just to show off to the other mums about how healthy they are). But, when I made the Penguin do a little penguin walk in Not-Lance's direction, he turned away. And I realised something. He looked miserable, and I didn't think it was *just* because of me. It was his dads. Clearly they were upsetting him. His name change told me that. So, was having *two* dads just as hard as having *none*? Was one dad the only number you should have? Or, perhaps, it was just having even numbers of dads that was bad. Perhaps three, five, seven, nine or eleven dads would be okay. Whatever it was I felt guilty, like my problems had taken over everything. I wished I could ask him but after lunch Miss Phillips put us in pairs.

And she put me with Billy Lee.

I stared in horror as the words came out of her mouth. *How could she do this to me?* Billy looked equally stunned, especially when Miss Phillips asked everyone else to leave the lunch room but told us to stay behind!

'Billy,' she said, when they were gone. 'You have something to say to Cymbeline, don't you?'

Billy stared down at his feet.

'But you didn't push his *shoes* into the swimming pool, did you? So you can say it to his *face*.'

Billy lifted his head like it was a boulder. I saw that his black eye wasn't actually black but a mixture of purple and green. They should be called purple and green eyes.

He mumbled, 'I'm sorry I pushed you in the swimming pool, Cymbeline.'

'Yeah, right you are.'

'I am,' he insisted and, weirdly, he looked like he meant it. That confused me and when Miss Phillips told us to catch up with the others I tapped him on the shoulder.

'Did you get *done* then?'

Billy nodded, and then faced forward as we hopped on to some escalators.

'Did Mrs Johnson call your mum?'

'Yeah.'

'From the office?'

He nodded again.

'And was she mad?'

'No.' Billy sighed. 'She wasn't there. My mum. She didn't answer her phone.'

'You are *so* lucky.'

'I'm *not*. Mrs Johnson, she . . .'

'What?'

His lips trembled. 'She called my dad. I begged her not to but she wouldn't listen. He was on site with clients and he had to come in and get me. He was so . . .'

'Mad?'

Billy just bit his lip instead of answering but I think he meant yes. I was about to ask what his dad did, but Marcus Breen tripped over at the top of the escalator and six of us fell over after him.

'This way please, St Saviour's,' the helper said.

We were going to see an exhibition. The painter's name was Munch; though, disappointingly, his first name was Edvard, not Monster. The helper gave us a talk about him and handed out sheets to the pairs, things we had to tick off. Billy and I looked at the paintings, which, unlike the Jackson Pollocks, were of actual people. People who were really bummed off. A woman was staring out across a lake like someone had just thrown her schoolbag in it. In another one this guy sitting on a bed looked like one of the Rotherham fans after Johnnie Jackson's winner. I wanted to tell him to cheer up but I couldn't of course and so my eyes found New Name Because Of New-Dad Boy instead. I wanted to tell him why I'd lied. How I'd *never* been swimming and how scared I was when Miss Phillips said we were going. I wanted to say I was sorry and that I couldn't wait until Saturday. I left Billy and walked over to him, but the helper called us in together and led us to one of the paintings.

When we were all sitting on the floor she told us that the painting we were looking at was Munch's most famous one. This was probably because the person in it looked even more miserable than the people in the other ones. The painting was called *The Scream* and was of this woman who was walking down a road towards the painter. 'Freaky' does not do enough to describe her. She had no proper face for a start, and there were these colours swirling around her head like Billy's multicoloured eye. She was screaming SO LOUD you could sort of hear her even though she was in a painting. The terrible thing, though, was that the people walking behind her were not miserable. They were laughing. And they couldn't see that she *was* miserable. The only person who could see that was you, the viewer – but you couldn't help her because you were outside the painting.

I stared, shaking my head, and then I looked at Lance again. And nodded. We *weren't* separate. We were in the same school, which meant that we *could* see each other and we did know how we were feeling. And – that being true – we *could* help each other.

Like friends do.

I stared at the picture until the helper asked who

would like to make a comment. I so wanted to say what I'd just thought, so that Lance could hear it too. My hand hit the sky but Veronique put hers up and so did Vi Delap and Elizabeth Fisher (though she just needed a wee). But the helper's eyes went behind us.

'Bradley,' she said, squinting at his nametag.

Bradley? We didn't have a Bradley. It was only when I turned round that I knew who she meant. So *that* was his new name.

'What does this painting make you think of?'

Bradley/Lance stood up and I nodded, knowing what he was going to say. It was what I'd been thinking too, that it looks like the secret pain we all carry around with us, and which we need our friends to share.

Wrong.

'It looks like Cym's mum,' Lance said. 'It looks just like his mum did at the swimming pool.'

There was silence.

Then someone giggled.

I don't know who.

Then that person started to snigger and someone else did. And then more. I don't know who laughed and who didn't. But there were a lot who did. Marcus Breen said, 'Yeah, that's your *mum*, Cymbeline.'

But though I heard it I didn't really hear it. Because I was moving. I didn't mean to move. This feeling in my stomach just sort of lifted me up towards Lance, who was laughing his head off at the reaction he'd got, but then he stopped. He looked worried. Then he looked scared as I launched myself towards him and pushed him over and then started to punch him really, *really*, *REALLY* hard.

CHAPTER TWELVE

Mrs Johnson called Auntie Mill from the office. Auntie Mill stormed in wearing a short white dress, trainers and this visor thing. Mrs Johnson said 'disgraceful' and 'shaming the whole school' and 'no excuse, whatever the situation at home,' and Auntie Mill so did not stick up for me. She just apologised for the behaviour of *her sister's son* and told me to sit in the car.

'And don't touch anything! Four–one to me in the deciding set and then you have to . . . Ooh!'

When we got to their house, she sent me up to the spare room and told me I had to stay there all night. It was yesterday's pizza for supper and Clay brought it up, pretending to be terrified when he passed me the plate. I ate it on the bed on my own and pushed the artichoke bits down the plughole. There wasn't any pudding.

Yesterday I'd been lonely. But now I felt terrible. Even looking at pictures of Mum on her tablet didn't make it any better. She didn't look like her somehow. She looked like my dad did on the mantelpiece. Just someone. Snizzling the fake Mr Fluffy didn't help either. I stared at the door, desperate for my mum. Knowing I couldn't have her I wanted to go downstairs instead and say I was sorry, *really* sorry. I just wanted to be with someone. Even if Juni or Clay didn't want to be with me, I'd join Auntie Mill on the sofa. I'd watch the cake programme, no problem, though had Auntie Mill seen *Incredible Edibles*? If she liked the cake thing, she might like that. I was about to go and ask her when there was this huge

WHACK!

on the bedroom window.

CHAPTER THIRTEEN

WHACK!

I stared at the turquoise curtains. It happened again.

WHACK!

I dived beneath the duvet and pulled it up to my chin.

What was happening? Were we under attack? I had no idea, though my first thought was that it might be Bradlance coming to get his own back. That was unlikely, however, and I had no idea who, or what, was outside. When the next whack came – even louder than the others – I knew that I had a choice. I could stay there, forever, hiding under the duvet like a big fat coward, or I could leap out, run over to the curtains and face the THING head on!

I stayed there under the duvet.

Then I stayed there some more. Then more, but the whacking didn't stop. I realised that Auntie Mill might hear it and come up and tell me off, and that was what forced me out of bed. I swallowed, and winced, then edged over to the window, picturing some hideous monster, all swirling eyes and dark colours like *The Scream*, with a head like Mrs Johnson's when she shouted at me. But when I finally plucked up the courage to peek through the curtains I saw . . .

A tennis ball.

The tennis ball was flying towards me, stopped by the window in front of my face before bouncing back towards a window in the house opposite.

Veronique caught it.

Veronique's house was really close to Auntie Mill's and Veronique was standing in her bedroom with the window open. The tennis ball was in her hand. She was about to throw it but she stopped when she saw me, and I just swallowed. When she signalled for me to open my window I did it, even though I was sure she was going to laugh at me for the swimming pool, or tell me I was crazy for what I'd done in the Tate. But instead she said, 'Are you going to the moon?'

I was not expecting that and I stared at her. But then I remembered that I was wearing my astronaut pyjamas, which Uncle Bill once got me from the Science Museum.

'I was just sitting here.'

'Who's that?' Veronique asked, her gaze moving to the teddy that was still in my hand.

'Not Mr Fluffy,' I said.

'Then what is he called?'

'No, that's his name. "Not Mr Fluffy".'

'That's a good name as he's not very fluffy, is he?'

'No,' I said. 'Though Mr Fluffy is.'

'Well, that's all right then.'

I put Not Mr Fluffy down and held my hands out. 'Go on then.'

'What?'

'Throw the ball. Didn't you want to play catch?'

'No, silly. That was just to get your attention.'

'Oh.'

'I want to come across.'

'Across?'

'Yes, a-cross,' Veronique said again, as if it should be very obvious.

'Across' was not obvious, but I soon found out what

113

it meant. Veronique stepped back into her room and reappeared with a metal ladder.

'It's for going up in our loft,' she explained. 'But it also works for this.'

This was pure madness and so

DO NOT DO THIS AT HOME.

Veronique slid the ladder out of her window until the near end was resting on my windowsill. After Veronique made sure that both ends were wedged in tight, she started crawling along it, across the gap between the two houses! I just stared, but when she held out her hand I pulled her in.

'Do you . . .? Do this a lot?'

Veronique jumped down. 'Juni and I used to all the time, though I don't think she likes me any more.'

'It's your lucky counter-ripostes.'

'Is that your mum?' Veronique said.

She was looking behind me, at Mum's tablet propped up on its stand on the bed. Before I could stop her she'd walked over and picked it up, staring hard at Mum's face. She looked serious, thoughtful, as if trying to work something out. Then she put it down and said, 'I've got something to show you.'

With that, Veronique skipped back to the window and out on to the ladder again. Not giving me a chance to ask questions she crawled back along it to her own room and then waved me to come over too. I swallowed, and stared back at the spare-room door, thinking about Auntie Mill. But I did it, my knees on the bars.

'Don't look down.'

What a stupid thing to say! I hadn't even thought of doing that but now I did and I swallowed at how far it was. I froze, unable to move, until Veronique said, 'Just imagine you're doing a space walk.'

That helped and eventually I made it to the other side

of the ladder, and then I was standing in Veronique's room. It was neat. No clothes out or curled-up pants on the floor. All the books were on the shelves. There were three done Rubik's Cubes and a stopwatch on a table by her bed. All this was pretty much as I might have pictured it, though her duvet surprised me. It had rabbits on and there was this big yellow elephant on her pillow.

'That's Cyrano,' she said. 'I got him from France. Where did you get Not Mr Fluffy?'

I had no idea and it made me wonder: where did the *real* Mr Fluffy come from?

'Is that what you wanted to show me?'

'No! This way,' Veronique said.

With that, she skipped out on to the landing and I followed. She led me down the stairs, and halfway down there was a window that I stopped at because through it I could see into Auntie Mill's house. I was relieved to see that she wasn't up in the spare room looking for me but right there on the sofa. I was more relieved to see that she was fast asleep, more lemonade on the table next to her.

'She'll be like that for hours,' Veronique said. 'Sometimes she's even there in the morning too.'

Veronique went on again and I followed, surprised by her house. The outside was about the same as Auntie Mill's but, inside, Auntie Mill's was one big room with bare white walls and shiny surfaces. It had spotlights in the ceilings and a staircase with no banisters. In contrast, Veronique's was old, with scruffy floorboards, paintings higgledy-piggledy and books piled up. At the bottom of the stairs her sword was hanging up with the coats and I wanted to have a go with it, but before I could ask she led me into the living room.

'Hi, *chérie*,' the woman said.

The woman – who had short brown hair – was sitting at a piano writing something on a pad in front of her. Veronique told her that I was Cymbeline and that I was staying next door. This information did not seem to faze her at all. She smiled and said she was Veronique's mum, and that Veronique had told her *a lot about me*.

I winced but Veronique laughed. '*Relax*. She doesn't mean about the swimming pool, do you, Mum?'

'No. Veronique tells me you're an *amazing* artist.'

She said that? 'Well, I . . .'

'Though I did tell her about the swimming pool, didn't I, Mum?'

I stared. 'You *did*?'

'But so what? It was only your penis, wasn't it?'

I blinked at her. 'My . . .?'

'Penis. That I saw. That we all saw. I mean, I know you've got one. Boys do. I've seen them before in books and in real life. And it wasn't a very different penis to the other ones. So you shouldn't be –'

'Veronique,' her mum said, 'perhaps you could take Cymbeline through to the kitchen.'

Veronique sighed but did as she was told. 'It's just *bodies*,' she muttered, leading me through. 'You're lucky *she's* got any clothes on. She often hasn't. We go to this beach in France on holiday where hardly anyone wears *any* clothes. There are penises everywhere. And vaginas of course. Hi, Dad.'

The back door had opened and a very thin man with straight black hair like Veronique's walked in. He said hi and – like Veronique's mum – didn't seem at all surprised to see a strange boy wearing astronaut pyjamas in their house. He just said I looked like the kind of fellow who liked pancakes. Something I said was TRUE. He poured batter into a pan, cooked the pancakes and then . . . SET FIRE TO THEM! This was almost as epic as they tasted. They were so good I forgot about what Veronique wanted to show me until she asked her dad a question.

'Can we go and see Nanai?'

'Wait until Cymbeline has finished his pancakes.'

'That's his fifth one, though.'

'Which means he has good taste. But have you had enough, Cymbeline?'

'Yeff fthank woo,' I said.

I finished my mouthful and Veronique carried our plates over. Wondering who, or what, Nanai was, I followed her out of the back door and down their garden, which had a trampoline but no goalposts. Veronique led me down to a little cottage with a glass door.

'That's Nanai,' she said, sliding the door open.

Nanai was curled up asleep in a big chair and I saw straightaway that she was a person. But not just any person. She was not just the oldest person I had ever *seen* in my life, but the oldest person I'd ever *imagined*. Her baggy skin folded down on to her like the person inside had been taken out. Her long white hair was so light it seemed to float around her head and her closed eyes looked like they hadn't opened in years, like a girl who goes to sleep in a fairy tale but actually gets older.

There were tiny drops of water on her eyelashes, like jewels.

'Is that your . . .?'

'Granny,' Veronique said. 'Nanai, to me. She's my dad's mum. Guess how old she is.'

'Four thousand.'

'Not quite. A hundred. How old's your granny?'

'No idea,' I said. 'Or my granddad. They live in Portugal now in somewhere my mum calls a retirement home for zombies, with golf. My other grandparents are dead. You're lucky to have Nanai.'

'I know.'

'Thanks for showing her to me.'

'It's not *her* I wanted to show you. It's these.'

Veronique walked past Nanai into the cottage and I followed, wondering if Nanai would wake up and say hello. She didn't and I stopped next to Veronique at a wall with lots of photographs. Veronique stared at them and I did too, seeing her in some, though she wasn't in the one she pointed to. That one showed a woman in a wide straw hat, holding hands with two little girls. Veronique put her finger on one.

'That's Nanai,' she said.

I turned to Nanai – still asleep – and then back to

the picture. Nanai looked about six, a little bit older than the other girl. I glanced back at her in the chair again and, weirdly, I did think I could recognise her.

'That's her mum with her,' Veronique said, pointing at the woman in the hat. 'And that's her twin sister, Thu. They were boat people.'

'You mean they could *float*?'

'No! They were like the refugees are today, from Libya, only she was Chinese, living in Vietnam. The Chinese were being murdered so they tried to flee across the ocean, in boats.'

'And did they?'

'Yes. Well, Nanai did. I don't know what happened to Thu and her mum. Anyway, that's Nanai when she was six and this is my dad when *he* was six.'

Veronique moved to the right and pointed at another picture. It showed a serious-looking woman who I could easily tell was Nanai. Next to her was a boy, and seeing him made me nervous. The woman was in a dress, but he was in swimming trunks.

'Dad tells me that Nanai was obsessed with swimming.'

I swallowed. 'With . . .?'

'Swimming, Cymbeline. For some reason Nanai

taught my dad to swim as soon as he was born. Then, when I was born, he taught me. He used to drop me in the swimming pool when I was a baby and let me come up on my own. Mum couldn't watch apparently but it's why I can swim well now. He taught me because his mum was obsessed with it. And he became obsessed with it too. Even now they make me do it.'

'You don't *like* swimming?'

'I do, but sometimes it's too much, what with everything else. I get no choice, though. Like you.'

'What?'

'But the other way round.'

'The other . . .?'

'You've *never* been taught, have you?'

I stared at Veronique. 'I . . .'

'You can't swim at all.'

'Whaaaaaat?' I laughed. 'Course I can. I just panicked because Billy pushed me in. I'm, like, *epic* at –'

'You cannot swim at all. Not one bit. I knew it when I pulled you out of the pool and I kept asking myself *how* could he *never* have gone swimming? *Everyone* goes swimming. I couldn't understand it until your mum went mad.'

'She did *not* go mad.'

'She did, though Lance shouldn't have said that. That was horrible. But she *did*. She's never taken you swimming, has she?'

There were tears at the back of my eyes. 'No.'

'And there's a reason for it. I could see that by the way she screamed at Miss Phillips. And it's really important to your mum. So what is it? Cymbeline, tell me – why has your mum *never* taken you swimming?'

CHAPTER FOURTEEN

I stared at Veronique as the question pounded in my head. *Why? All those stupid excuses.* Sand, crocodiles, the Loch Ness monster. It was like a sheet had fallen away from in front of me. They weren't true. I could see that now. They were just things you say to a two-year-old. I'd believed them and then just, somehow, *carried on believing them.*

Or had I?

I shook my head because no, I hadn't, not really. I knew there was a real reason. But Mum got *so upset* about swimming that I'd always pretended it was nothing. But it wasn't nothing; it was something big, and real, and most of all something I couldn't turn away from. Not now. Not after what had happened.

My going in the swimming pool meant that Mum was in hospital, and I had to find out the truth: for *her*.

I had to find it out for Mum.

But how?

Veronique kissed Nanai's forehead and then we walked back up to her house.

'Thank your dad for the pancakes,' I said, stepping back out of her bedroom on to the ladder. 'And your mum for having her clothes on.'

I crawled over and climbed on the bed as Veronique pulled the ladder back. Veronique's words about swimming were still ringing in my brain and I felt weird, sort of naked. The reason . . . The *real* reason. How could I find out what it was?

The answer came when I picked up Not Mr Fluffy and stared into his shiny eyes.

I'd gone back to get him, hadn't I?

I'd gone back home, for him, my pyjamas and Mum's tablet.

So why couldn't I go back again?

For the answer.

Three minutes later I was dressed. Taking short sharp breaths, I tiptoed down the stairs, half wanting Auntie Mill to be awake so that I could back out of this. When I saw that she was still asleep I pushed on, though outside the back door I had to pause behind a hedge. Clay wasn't in his room like I'd thought but climbing up into the treehouse. Ha! If he thought there were any sweets in that Tupperware box he was going to be disappointed. When he was inside I took a deep breath, scuttling round to the front of the house, stopping only when Veronique stuck her head out of her window.

'Where are you going?' she hissed.

'Home,' I replied.

Veronique asked why, but I ignored her, knowing that she could easily talk me out of it. I also knew that instead of doing that she might ask to come too, and, much as I wanted her to, something told me that I had to do this on my own, though when I got out on to the road I nearly changed my mind.

It was soooo scary.

I'd never been out on my own in the daylight, let alone at night. It all looked different. It wasn't just dark, which of course I'd seen. The trees looked bigger, looming over me and shaking their leaves like people laughing, and not in a good way. The people walking past looked different too, like they were made out of harder stuff than normal. And there were NO KIDS. Not *one*, like in *Chitty Chitty Bang Bang* in the castle, when they've all been stolen or hidden. I swallowed, keeping my eye out for the Child Catcher as I forced myself to push on into Blackheath Village, where there were even more people, who all seemed to be on their phones, giving me the weird thought that they were talking about me and that any second a police car would zoom up and I'd be grabbed.

I shivered and told myself not to be stupid, but actually an adult *might* wonder what a nine-year-old was doing out on his own at night. Not wanting anyone to ask me, I looked around, catching sight of an old couple walking their dog. I hurried up and walked behind them, hoping that people would assume I was with them, which they seemed to do. I followed the couple past the train station, then up past the Costa, towards the heath.

I was calmer now, though I knew I had to be quiet or they'd turn round and see me. I followed them up towards the Hare and Billet pub, hoping they'd go up along the heath road towards my house, but they didn't – up near school they turned away and I hesitated, seeing more people coming towards me.

Taking another deep breath I left the path and headed across the middle of the dark heath, where there would be no one to question me. It was creepy and the heath seemed twice as big as usual, but I got to the other side eventually. I was relieved, though I also knew what I'd have to tackle then.

A ROAD.

I'd crossed two roads already – but that was right behind the dog walkers. And this one was different: I was *alone*. I had *never* crossed a road alone before. I looked around for more dog walkers but there weren't any and so I bit my lip and crossed my fingers. Then, like Billy at the swimming pool, I edged up to the kerb until my toes were sticking out. I stuck my neck out and looked LEFT.

Nothing coming.

This was a relief and so I did the same thing again – but looking RIGHT. There was nothing coming that way either and, happier now, I got ready to cross, but before doing so I stopped. I'd looked LEFT and there was nothing coming, but what if something had *started* to come along from the LEFT when I was looking RIGHT? As fast as I could I looked LEFT again and there was nothing coming, but now I had the same problem but from the other direction: what if something had started to come from the RIGHT after I'd stopped looking RIGHT and was looking LEFT? In fact, how could I ever be sure that nothing was coming from one way when I was looking the other way? I looked LEFT again, trying to do it so fast that I could sort of look RIGHT at the same time but it didn't work. Drat. There was nothing for it, though, and so eventually I crossed, amazed to find myself on the other side with my legs and arms still attached.

Three minutes later I was outside my house. (I'd walked down Morden Hill and crossed another road, though this one had a pelican crossing so it was okay.) Then, staring at my door, I stopped, suddenly realising what I was doing. I was going into my house – at *night*, on my *own* – to find something out about my mum. Something she hadn't wanted me to know because, if she had, she would have told me, wouldn't she? I clenched my fists and had the same odd feeling that I'd had when looking at her photograph: that this was just a house, that it was separate from me and strange. I nearly turned round but I couldn't, so without thinking I forced my hand into my bag and pulled out the key. Then I unlocked the door and pushed it open.

The house was dark. As quickly as I could I found the light switch, which is when the strange feeling vanished. Because I was looking at my home. At our home. I thought about Auntie Mill's house, which was huge, but I shook my head because I wasn't jealous one bit. This was *our* house, where *we* lived, and though it was a bit battered and you couldn't get the ice cream out of the freezer, and my bedroom door didn't close properly, I loved it.

More cheerful now, I walked into the living room and began. I looked in the big cabinet the telly sits on. I looked behind the sofa and on the mantelpiece, finding 37p and Park Lane (from Monopoly) but no clues about why Mum had never taken me swimming. There was nothing in the hall either or in the kitchen. Up in the bathroom there was nothing unusual except for two dead spiders and an old toothpaste tube under the chest of drawers. I was more hopeful in the boxroom and I went into bags and opened suitcases, finding loads of old clothes, though not the checked shirt my dad was wearing in the picture on the mantelpiece. There were some papers in a file and I stared at some more photos of my dad, black-and-white ones with his name on, him looking serious. Underneath were some photographs of me as a baby, some in various baby-gros, a few with nothing on and a couple of baby me and baby Lance. I didn't want to look at those so I put them down and then sighed, really disappointed because there was nothing about swimming – and that meant there was only one place left to look.

And I didn't want to look in there.

There wouldn't be anything in my room – Mum was hardly likely to leave something in my room that she didn't want me to know about. So that just left *her* room.

Are you scared of your parents' bedroom? Or, not scared, exactly, but you just know that there's something *different* about it? Compared to the other rooms in your house? If so, you'll understand how I felt as I stood on the landing and stared at Mum's door. I really did not want to go in there. To begin with she wouldn't be there and that felt odd, though she goes in my room without me all the time.

'Cymbeline,' she'd said once. She'd taken me upstairs and was pointing into my bedroom. 'Very tidy in here, isn't it?'

I knew there was something different. 'Yes!'

'But half an hour ago it wasn't tidy. It was a

complete disaster. Do you know how it got tidy?'

I thought really hard about that. But I had to give up. I shrugged and Mum frowned. 'Elves, do you think?'

'Come on, Mum, there's no such thing as elves.'

'Goblins then?'

'Same thing, and they're evil anyway. They so would not tidy up a bedroom.'

'Agreed. So how did it happen?'

'Nope, sorry.'

'Shall I tell you?'

'If you like, though no stress if you don't want to.'

'It was me, Cymbeline. *I* picked up all the things *you* just threw about the place and *completely forgot about. I* did it, okay?'

'Okay,' I said. 'And thanks very much for telling me that, Mum.'

So it was fine to go in her room without her – but I still didn't want to. I didn't want to look in her cupboards or her drawers, and then there was the Art End.

There are two halves to Mum's room. The nearest half has her bed in and I'm allowed in there of course, though on Sunday mornings I have to wait until seven thirty. I used to come in earlier but Mum taught me

134

how to tell the time so I wouldn't any more. The other half is where Mum does her art. Not *all* her art because we do loads at the kitchen table together. But this is her private art, not connected with the workshops she runs or anything. She does this on Friday afternoons with no one else in the house, and it's OFF LIMITS. Looking in there would get me into real trouble and I so hoped I'd find some sort of answer in the near half.

But there was nothing in her bedside drawers apart from bras that looked like sleeping animals, and squashed-up pants, T-shirts and skirts and pairs of jeans. There was nothing in the wardrobe either, apart from jackets and dresses, including the one from Oxfam she doesn't wear any more. Or was there? Reaching my hand forward, I felt cold. Then, reaching further, I felt even colder and, stepping up and into the wardrobe, I felt something beneath my feet, something soft and crunchy. Peering forward, through Mum's dresses, I saw a lamppost up ahead of me.

Only joking. I shut the wardrobe and turned round. And then there I was, staring at the Chinese birds on the folding screen that Mum bought from the junk shop in Greenwich, which separates one side of her room from the other. I took a deep breath, thinking of Jackson Pollock, the colours inside me no longer lined up but mad, and whirling, and wrong. And, thinking of those paintings, I wondered for the first time ever what Mum's would be like. I knew it was paintings – not sculptures or collages – because she was always getting paint from the art shop near Greenwich station. But did she paint old people? Or miserable people? Did she just do masses of scribbles, or put triangles next to squares, or do shadows that made the whole world look sad? I didn't know. And there was no point trying to guess. So I pulled the screen aside, and was amazed.

Ghosts. Lots of them. That's what I thought at first, though it wasn't ghosts. It was sheets, covering the paintings, and at first I couldn't bring myself to pull them off – because why tell me not to look in here if it was okay for me to see what she did? *And*, I suddenly thought, *what if these paintings have something to do with my dad? Why he died.* But I had to look at them, I knew it, and I pulled the sheets off and stared, totally and utterly stunned by what I saw.

The paintings were big. All of them. They were big and rectangular and there were lots of them, on easels or the floor, each one staring back at me, and every one the same. All of them. Every single painting was identical to the one next to it.

Exactly. The. Same.

CHAPTER FIFTEEN

And every single one was of Mr Fluffy.

CHAPTER SIXTEEN

We lost him once. On Juni's seventh birthday (I was six). Juni had always wanted to go on an open-top bus round London. Clay was there and Auntie Mill and Uncle Chris (Clay and Juni's dad) and I was and Mum, and Uncle Brian came too. We climbed the stairs up to the top deck and sat next to these American people, who had coats on even though it was summer, and more teeth than English people. I sat next to Juni and she told me all about London as we drove around. For instance, when we got to the Tower of London, she said it wasn't really called that. The Tower of London was actually the name of the bell inside it, and its real name was St Stephen's Tower. She knows so much stuff, Juni, which probably comes from going to her different school.

We saw the London Eye, which I thought only looked worth going on if it went faster. At Buckingham Palace the Queen was out because there was no flag, and this was disappointing for some reason, even though we wouldn't have been able to see her anyway. Auntie Mill said they should have a flag at their house for when Uncle Chris was home, though they'd hardly ever have to put it up, would they? Uncle Chris laughed at that, sort of, and came to sit with me and Juni. At the Houses of Parliament he tried to point out the Burghers of Calais in a little park but I couldn't see any burgers (though we did pass a few McDonald's). The Americans all got off but we stayed on until Trafalgar Square, where Juni wanted to climb on the lions. We all got off and did that, and I looked up at Nelson, all lonely on his column. I wanted to bring his statue down to the ground so he could be surrounded by all the people he'd saved. Uncle Chris said that Nelson had captured the lions from Napoleon and I said that was great but why did he make them so slippery?

We looked at a very still person pretending to be Yoda and a very still person pretending to be Darth Vader and a very still person pretending to be Gandalf and they were good, but not as good as the very still person pretending to be a soldier near Buckingham Palace. He'd looked more real because he had his own hut and his face wasn't covered in paint.

Back on the bus Mum said, 'Photo time!'

We squashed in together but her eyes went wide. 'Where's Mr Fluffy?' she said.

I felt suddenly empty as I scrabbled behind me on the seat and on the floor. We all ran down the stairs, and Mum begged the driver to let us off before the next stop. We ran back into the square, looking near the lions and the still people and by the fountain and *everywhere*.

I was desperate, but I wasn't as bad as Mum, and she was the one who spotted him. He was with a kid! The kid was about my age and was holding him. Mum ran in front of him and the kid's mum and I saw her speaking, obviously asking for Mr Fluffy back. I thought – *doh* – that the mum would just hand him over, but she started to argue, saying something about *proving* it was *hers*. Eventually Mum gave up arguing and just grabbed Mr Fluffy, and the other mum got really angry. She pushed Mum and then, suddenly, a policeman turned up. Not a pretending one, a real one! The woman wanted to report Mum for pushing her kid, which she hadn't, and it all got serious until Uncle Chris went over. He managed to sort it out, but Auntie Mill hissed at Mum that it was just a *teddy bear for heaven's sake* and *Juniper's only seven once* and *why do you always ruin things?* Then they started arguing.

'Why do Mum and Auntie Mill fight all the time?' I asked Uncle Brian, when we were back on the bus. He blew his cheeks out and I could tell there were loads of thoughts in his head, though all he would say in the end was, '*Sisters.*'

Mum kept hold of Mr Fluffy all the way home.

And all this time, for some reason, she's been painting loads of pictures of him.

I stared at Mr Fluffy for what seemed like ages, until it looked in fact like he was staring back at me. I looked around at the rug he was sitting on and at the other things in the picture, until a police siren going past seemed to sort of wake me up. I covered all the pictures up again, and hurried back to Auntie Mill's.

In the morning, after breakfast, Auntie Mill walked me round to Veronique's house. Her mum was going to take me to school. Veronique pulled me inside, put away her violin, and asked me what I'd found at home. I told her (after saying how totally scary it was walking through Blackheath and how, coming back, Auntie Mill nearly caught me climbing up the stairs). She asked why my mum had painted just Mr Fluffy and I said I had no idea, so she asked me to describe the paintings. I tried but it was really hard with words – I wanted to *show* her, and it wasn't long before I got the chance.

At school, before register, Miss Phillips came up to me and I thought she was going to roast my ears again about the Tate. Instead she said she knew that I was having a *bit of trouble* at home. And because of that, after assembly, she had something different for me. For a second I thought she meant taking me to see Mum, but she didn't. As the rest of Year 4 filed back into our classroom Miss Phillips jerked her head at me, then led me into the room where after-school computer club normally is. Inside I saw that the tables had been rearranged into a big square, and a man who I'd never seen before was standing by them. Miss Phillips told me he was Mr Prentice and that he did something called 'art therapy'.

'Is that making people in Munch pictures look happier?'

He laughed, scratching his big ginger beard. 'No, we're going to hang out for a bit. And make stuff.'

'What sort of stuff?'

'Anything. Veronique will show you if you like.' The man smiled and looked over my shoulder. 'She comes every week, don't you, Veronique?'

Veronique walked in, while I frowned. I knew she missed class on Thursday mornings, but I'd always thought it was to go off and do genius things, like extra maths or science. Why did *she* need to come here? She's super clever, can swim really well, and has an even number of parents.

'Why do you need therapy?' I asked.

'It helps me calm down a bit. Mr Prentice says it's because he doesn't ever give a mark or anything. It's relaxing. So Miss Phillips lets me come.'

'To do art?'

'Yes, though last week I did Mr Prentice's tax return.'

'You weren't supposed to mention that, Veronique,' the man said. 'Now then, Cymbeline. What do *you* fancy doing?'

I tried not to sound too keen but I didn't need to think about it. I asked for some paint and a big sheet of paper, Veronique asking if she could just watch me that week. Mr Prentice said fine, and I began painting Mr Fluffy to show Veronique what Mum had done in her pictures.

It was hard. For a start, I didn't have her painting in front of me like I'd had with Jackson Pollock at the Tate – Mum's were too big to carry back to Auntie Mill's. Also, in Mum's paintings, Mr Fluffy was wearing a T-shirt. Mr Fluffy doesn't actually *have* a T-shirt, but Mum had painted him in one. There was writing on it but I'd have to wait until the paint dried before I added it or it would smudge. Instead, once I'd finished Mr Fluffy and told Veronique who he was, I started on the picnic rug, which Mum had painted him sitting on. I should have done that first of course but I managed to make it look okay – blue-and-white check.

'That's from Decathlon,' said Veronique. 'We've got the same one.'

There were two paper drinks cups on the rug too, and I did those. They'd fallen over next to Mr Fluffy, so I also did the coffee stains on the white bits of the rug. Something made me stop then and think of Mum in the hospital.

Two sugars. Two sugars.

Did that have something to do with *this*?

I carried on, doing my best to remember Mum's pictures. I added the shadows from Mr Fluffy and the cups, and Veronique grabbed hold of my arm.

'Midday,' she said.

'What?'

'The time. We copied De Chirico paintings at the Tate and his were in the afternoon; you could tell because of the shadows. But these shadows are tiny so it must be near midday.'

I shrugged, not knowing what that really told us, and carried on painting some red flip-flops on the rug and a little beaker like a baby uses for water. Next to them I put a scrunched-up brown ball.

Veronique's finger flew out to it. 'What's that?'

'Paper,' I said. 'Though it's hard to do.'

'What sort of paper?'

'No idea. For sandwiches maybe?'

'But where are the sandwiches?'

'Maybe someone ate them.'

'Then why didn't they put the paper in the bin?'

'How do I know? Maybe they were in a hurry or something.'

'I still think you should put litter in the bin,' Veronique said.

I agreed and got on with the picture, adding another screwed-up piece of paper next to the other one before remembering the rug's tassels. After them I did the grass around it, which was quite long and had daisies and buttercups here and there. After that I did a thin slice at the top of the picture where Mum had painted a pathway, with people walking dogs on it, or in bright clothing going past on bikes. I put the brush down and looked at what I'd done.

'Very *good*,' Mr Prentice said, looking up from his phone. 'I mean, really. But aren't you going to finish it?'

'I have.'

'But what about that bit?' he insisted, pointing at a big section in the upper half of the picture.

I'd left that part blank. I hadn't touched it at all. But I couldn't put anything there because Mum hadn't either. She'd painted Mr Fluffy on a rug – over and over – but she'd left almost all of the top third of every single painting blank. You could see Mr Fluffy, and the rug, and the grass, and a little path at the top, but you couldn't see anything else.

'Did she run out of time?' Veronique asked, but I shook my head.

'She can't have. She went on to the next painting, didn't she?'

'So what was in that bit then?'

I had no idea, and it was really frustrating. I'd gone all the way home through the night to find out about Mum. What I'd discovered was that she liked painting Mr Fluffy. What did *that* tell me about the swimming pool? I was disappointed. I'd hoped that doing the painting myself, in the daytime, might make me see something new about it that I hadn't seen the night before. But nothing came.

'She only painted this?' Veronique asked.

'I told you.'

'Then it must mean something. Your mum took Mr Fluffy to the hospital, so he must be connected to what happened with Billy at the pool.'

'I suppose.'

'And so must this place.'

'This place?'

'Where the rug is of course.'

I turned back to the painting and realised that Veronique was right, though I hadn't thought about that at all. I'd just focused on the fact that it was Mr Fluffy, but the rug had to be *somewhere*. Veronique leaned forward and squinted at the picture.

'Where *is* this, Cymbeline?'

That question obsessed me for the rest of the day. I thought about it as I helped Veronique with her project, something called DNA that she was making out of little straws. She told me what DNA was and I stared at her.

'There are billions of straws inside us?'

'Oh, Cymbeline!' Veronique said.

I thought about it at lunch, sitting next to the climbing wall in the playground with Veronique, so focused on the problem that I didn't quite realise how amazing it felt just to be doing that. We stared at the painting for ages.

'It's not the city.'

'It could be a park. Her hospital's in a park.'

'No, the grass is too long. But it's not exactly countryside either.'

'Why not?'

'Because it has to be somewhere they sell coffee, doesn't it?'

She was right but it didn't get us any further. We stared and stared but there was no way we could know any more that that. Veronique said she wished she'd seen Mum's paintings herself and I got angry because my version showed *everything*.

Veronique sighed. 'Then I wish she'd finished it!' she said, before going off to lunchtime music club. I stayed where I was and wished that too, wondering *why* Mum had never shown me her paintings if this was all they showed. *And* why she'd put Mr Fluffy in a T-shirt. I squinted at him and shook my head because I'd forgotten to add the writing, hadn't I? I'd have to do it later. I squeezed my mind up and saw the words from Mum's paintings again.

Eglinhs Hretigae.

I had no idea what they meant.

CHAPTER SEVENTEEN

It was no good – the painting just wasn't going to tell me anything. So there was only one thing left to do.

I had to see my mum.

I had to just ask her: what is your thing about swimming really about?

But how could I get to the hospital?

That problem vexed me all afternoon. I couldn't concentrate on the video about the Romans that Miss Phillips showed us, and I didn't even care about tag rugby in PE, which I'd been looking forward to ever since Year 1. The trouble was, Uncle Bill, who had taken me last time, was away. Maybe I could go on my own? I'd gone home on my own, hadn't I? But that was at night. I'd have to go to the hospital in the day, and someone would miss me, either school or Auntie Mill. The only way I could think of was to get Auntie Mill to take me herself, but she was still 'livid' with me for getting called by Mrs Johnson when she was 4–1 up.

When she picked me up, I decided to say I was really sorry about that and promise to be really good – if she'd take me. But Juni was with her and I didn't get the chance because Juni talked all the way home: some girl in her class had said *this*, while some other girl had said *that*, which meant that some other girl, again, had said *something else*, which had started yet another girl crying, which led to the first girl saying the first thing all over again. I didn't interrupt because I thought it would be easier back at theirs. I'd get Auntie Mill on her own when Juni and Clay went off to their rooms.

Except they didn't. Juni dumped her bag on the floor and slumped down on the sofa.

'Aren't you going on your PS4?' I asked. Juni raised her eyes and did this big exaggerated sigh.

'Not on *Thursdays*.'

'Oh, why not?'

'Because *Thursdays* is "*family time*".'

When I asked what that was, Juni didn't answer.

Instead she put her hands round her neck and pretended to strangle herself, her tongue sticking out until she fell over sideways into the cushions. Auntie Mill explained for her. On Thursdays, said Auntie Mill, computers weren't allowed. On Thursdays they got a takeaway and *did things together.* In contrast to the face Juni was making, Auntie Mill sounded very jolly about it, though the first thing they all did that Thursday was have a massive argument about the takeaway.

Clay came in and wanted fish and chips. Juni, however, said that if they got that she would vomit. I mean, *so totally.* She wanted something called soo-shee but Clay said he'd rather eat her vomit than eat that. Doing my best to be nice to Auntie Mill, I said *she* should choose and she shouted yes! Why not for ONCE? But when she suggested Indian food Juni and Clay said they would *both* vomit, so she ended up ordering soo-shee from one place and fish and chips from another. That really should have made them both happy but Juni simply could not believe that Auntie Mill had forgotten to order tempura prawns, and asked if she was going senile.

Clay stared at his peas.

'They're not mushy!' he cried.

Auntie Mill went off to get herself some lemonade after that, and then it was time to argue about the board game. Clay said Juni's choice (Cluedo) was for stupid little stupid babies and Juni said that the only thing more boring than Risk was death. Clay said he'd arrange for her to play that if she liked and I thought Juni was going to attack him, so again I said Auntie Mill should choose.

'Yes, why not?! Monopoly then.'

'Great,' I said. 'I've got Park Lane!'

'But that's not FAIR!' Juni said. 'If he's already got Park Lane before we even start, I'M NOT PLAYING!!'

I explained that I just happened to have it in my pocket but we didn't start quite then anyway. Juni called dibs on being the little dog and Clay cut her eyebrow when he threw it at her.

Auntie Mill went to get some plasters and more lemonade and I followed her into the kitchen.

'What is it?' she hissed when she heard me behind her. 'Do I have to take Juniper to accident and emergency because Clayton's shoved the Chance cards down her throat?'

'No,' I said. 'I was just wondering . . .'

'If you can be the dog? Oh, *please* –'

'No,' I cut in. 'I'll be the boot. That's fine. I was just wondering if you would take me to see my mum tomorrow?'

Auntie Mill was cutting up a lemon on their island thing. She had her back to me. She stopped still and let out a breath.

'No,' she said.

I stared at her. 'But why not? Is it because of Lance?'

'Lance?'

'The boy I hit?'

'What? No. Not that. I mean, yes, I'm still cross, my serve was really firing and . . . never mind. Cymbeline, it's still too early. We just have to wait.'

'But how do you *know* that?'

'Because,' Auntie Mill said, turning round to face me, 'I went there.'

I hadn't expected that, and my mouth went dry. I tried to swallow but I couldn't. 'When?' I said.

'I went there this morning.'

'This . . .? And . . .' I could hardly even ask. 'How *is* she?'

Auntie Mill shrugged. 'I don't know, do I?'

'You don't *know*?'

'No. Because I went all the way over there only to

be told that she wouldn't see me. In fact, it was written down: *I* wasn't allowed in. Nor would the doctor discuss her condition with me. Confidential, he said, and here I am looking after her son while –'

'But she'd want to see me,' I said.

Auntie Mill blinked. 'What do you mean?'

'Well. It's . . . just you. Because . . .'

'Yes?'

'You argue all the time.'

Auntie Mill slammed her hands on to her hips and her eyes flew open. 'We do *not*.'

'You do. Even when you're not arguing you still sort of are.'

'Well, that's just because we're sisters.'

'Is it? Is it really?' I said.

I'm not sure what made me say that but Auntie Mill paused. Her eyes seemed to shiver and she nodded, just a little, as if to say, 'Okay, you asked for it.' She turned aside to glug a drink called Gordon's into her lemonade then looked down at me again.

'I used to be an actor.'

'What?' It certainly wasn't what I was expecting. 'You mean like on *Hank Zipzer*?'

'Yes, though I did theatre mostly.'

'I see.' Did I? What did that have to do with arguing with my mum, *or* taking me to see her?

'I was in a play,' Auntie Mill went on.

'Was it about sisters then?'

'No.'

'Well then . . . what . . .?'

'It was by Shakespeare, *Cymbeline*. And there was this man in it.'

'One of the dead ones who's still breathing?'

'One of the other actors. I *liked* him. I *really* liked him, actually. And he liked me.'

'So what happened?'

'Age-restricted content. But your mum came to see the play one night. I can still see her, all artsy and Bohemian-looking. And afterwards, well, *she* decided to like him too.'

'You mean . . .?'

'Your dad, Cymbeline. Yes. And – *of course* – he liked her too, didn't he?'

'Blimey. Were you cross?'

'Oh, just a little bit, you might say.'

'Wow. I get it. But why are you still cross with Mum now?'

'*Now?*'

'Yes. I mean, you've got Uncle Chris now, haven't you?'

'Oh yes,' Auntie Mill said, her voice going suddenly quiet, 'I've got Uncle *Chris*, haven't I? And that makes everything all right, doesn't it?'

With that, Auntie Mill grabbed her drink and marched into the living room.

I followed, but I was so angry. There was nothing else I could do to get to see Mum and there was only one reason – I was just a kid. I was a kid and I needed an adult to do things. It was so frustrating and I wanted to scream at Auntie Mill, ask her why she couldn't understand. I got this real stab of hatred for her, like I'd swallowed a Fab whole and it had got stuck in my chest. I hated Uncle Bill too – for not being there – and then, making my stomach turn over, I hated someone else. Mum. For leaving me. How could she do that? No matter what? Didn't she know what would happen to me, how much I'd miss her and worry, how – yes – I'd be like Oliver Twist, in spite of the nice house I was in. Worse than him in fact because his mum had died; she hadn't gone off on purpose. It didn't last, though. Mum couldn't help what had happened. She was ill. It wasn't her fault. And then the hatred was replaced by a gush of love that was almost painful because – as bad as I was feeling – she must be feeling worse. At least I had my aunt and my cousins, didn't I? Who did she have?

I wasn't into the Monopoly. I actually did get Park Lane and then Mayfair, though no one landed on them. No one ever does, do they? I was out first and mumbled goodnight, no one paying attention really because they were into it now. I picked up my bag and trudged up the stairs, picking up Mum's tablet from the bed. I woke it up, once again desperate to connect with her, but she only smiled back for a second. The battery died and I stared at the black screen, which seemed right somehow because I'd run out of ideas. Out of everything. There was nothing left, nothing else I could think of, and I wouldn't even be able to talk about it with Veronique tomorrow. Miss Phillips had reminded us that tomorrow was an Inset Day, which meant we didn't have to go to school. Veronique was the only person I could talk to really, and with all the extra classes she did at the weekends I probably wouldn't even see her until Monday.

I got into bed. I snizzled Not Mr Fluffy, but there was no point. He just wasn't Mr Fluffy. You can't ever replace anyone with someone else. It doesn't work. I pushed him aside but felt bad because of course it wasn't his fault. It was me, trying to make him be what he wasn't. I snizzled him again and it was okay, so I closed my eyes and changed his name to Not Mr Fluffy (But Teddy In His Own Right), and I was about to fall asleep when it

An Inset Day.

A day on which I didn't have to go to school.

A day on which no one at school would miss me if I *wasn't there*.

A day on which Auntie Mill would have to look after me.

What if – *somehow* – and by *mistake* of course, through absent-mindedness, or worry about my mum and Lance, and totally not on *purpose*, I sort of, tum-tee-tum, *accidentally*, FORGOT TO TELL HER ABOUT IT?

CHAPTER EIGHTEEN

In the morning I got dressed in my school uniform. I went downstairs and took the Weetabix out of the cupboard. I could hear Auntie Mill in the back room and I waited for her to come through, intending to tell her that Veronique's mum would be taking me to school again. Auntie Mill would be pleased and I'd leave the house, pretending I was going next door. But I'd walk to Blackheath station. No one would stop me in the daytime. I'd go down to the same platform I'd gone to with Uncle Bill and get on a train to Welling. I'd walk past the charity shops and then the Greggs, and then through the park to the hospital. I'd managed to get inside last time, hadn't I? I wouldn't be worried about seeing her. She'd had enough time to get better surely and even if she wasn't totally well, just seeing me would cheer her up. I'd sprint round to Mum's ward and throw myself into her arms and then ask her about her paintings.

But Auntie Mill said, 'Morning, Cymbeline. Any idea what you want to do today?'

I stared at her. She was wearing that short white dress again with the visor thing, and she was carrying a huge bag.

'Er, maths. I'm really looking forward to that. And RE.'

'What?'

'At school of course.'

'But didn't you know? You're off today.'

'I'm . . .?'

'Off. All day. Aren't you pleased?'

I sighed, not even wondering how she'd found out about the Inset Day. I just said yes, sure, slumping down into myself, a sort of fuzzy greyness filling me up with the failure of my last plan. The only thing that stopped it was confusion: Auntie Mill was humming to herself. Weirdly, she looked *cheerful*, even though she was going to have to look after me all day. Did that mean I was just going to have to follow her around, watching what she was doing? I was about to ask but she turned away and set an envelope with 'Chris' written on it next to the kettle before looking at her watch. And then an odd thing happened. The doorbell rang and Veronique walked in – with her mum. Behind them were two more people – Billy Lee and *his* mum. I stared, remembering that Veronique had said that Billy lived near them, and I watched as both mums thanked Auntie Mill and left. This was even more weird because the addition of two extra children didn't seem to worry Auntie Mill at all. I couldn't fathom it until she opened the back door.

'Bye then,' she said. 'Have fun.'

My eyes opened. 'You're . . . *leaving*?'

'What? Oh, yes. Busy day.'

'So we'll be . . . on our own?'

'What? No, of course not. You'll be –'

Auntie Mill didn't finish because, at that moment, something else unexpected happened. I got this really strong smell that was sort of like metal flowers, and Uncle Chris hurried in. I hadn't even realised he was there. He must have got back from Zurich last night after I fell asleep. Auntie Mill paused at the door and we all watched him talking very quickly on his phone while doing his tie up at the same time. And it was funny – it was like he was in a sort of tunnel. He didn't seem to *see* Auntie Mill, or any of us, not even after he'd done his tie up and ended his phone call. He just grabbed his watch from the side and strapped it on, reminding me of the last time I'd seen him because he'd wanted to show it to me.

'See. The second hand. Continuous motion. Sweeps round without stopping.'

'You mean, it doesn't tick?'

'Nope.'

'What a shame,' I'd said. 'Maybe you can get your money back.'

When the watch was on, Uncle Chris hurried over to the door, only then noticing Auntie Mill. His eyes then landed on me.

'Riiight!' he said. 'Yes. Cym-bo. Heard you were here. How goes it, old soldier? These your chums, yes?'

'I am,' Veronique said. 'But not him. They hate each other.'

'Great,' said Uncle Chris, giving us a thumbs-up.

With that, Uncle Chris turned back to Auntie Mill and smiled with his mouth shut, nodding at her, clearly expecting her to step out of the way so that he could dash out through the door. But – instead – she dashed through the door herself! And then she rammed it shut behind her! This seemed to confuse Uncle Chris because he stared at her.

'Lo-ove?' he said, reaching for the handle. 'Mind if I just get past? So got to scoot. *Whopper* day.'

'Cymbeline doesn't like artichoke,' said Auntie Mill from the other side of the door.

This stopped Uncle Chris, and his mouth dropped open. 'He doesn't like . . .?'

'Artichoke. Hates them. Just so you know.'

'Great. Saved to the hard drive. But why do I *need* to know?'

'Because you've got him today. And his friends.'

Uncle Chris blinked. 'I've . . .?'

'Didn't you get my text? Inset Day. Anyway, have fun!'

'*What?!*'

'Look, love, I would chat but Zac *really hates it* when I'm late.'

'*Zac?*'

'Gets quite shirty actually. He's doing great things with my backhand but I *need* the court time. You don't grudge me do you, love? I mean, I've had the kids every day for, hmmm, now let me *see*, what is it, *thirteen years* now? Juni's gone in with Clay, so you don't have to worry about that, though you'll have to pick them up later of course. But meanwhile you've got these three. *Bye now.*'

'WAIT!' screamed Uncle Chris.

Uncle Chris then tried to pull the door open but he couldn't – Auntie Mill had locked it from the outside. It took him a while to get it open with the spare key, by which time Auntie Mill had gone round to the front. Uncle Chris ran after her and we all followed as he screamed words like 'Brexit', 'liquidity' and 'meltdown' – followed by two of the words I'd heard at Charlton. Not that he should have bothered, though – Auntie Mill couldn't hear. Her car was already halfway up the road, the sight of which made Uncle Chris shout the third Charlton word three times in a row. And then he turned to us.

'Get in,' he bellowed.

For a second I thought he meant the house, but he didn't. Uncle Chris meant his car, which was parked on the driveway right in front of us, though you might not have noticed it if you weren't looking. Like Auntie Mill's it's very shiny, but there's something about rich people's cars: they're either very high or *extremely* low. Uncle Chris's barely came up to my knees, making me wonder if it would fit any actual people. We all did manage to squash in, though: me in the front and Veronique and Billy in the back. And we were OFF, the feeling as we zoomed up the road just like when Billy had shoved me in the back.

At the end of the road Uncle Chris rammed the brakes on, jerking his head both ways as he searched in vain for Auntie Mill. Then he slammed his fists into the steering wheel.

'Cymbo,' he said, 'where does your auntie play tennis?'

'I don't know,' I said, fighting for breath because the seatbelt was trying to strangle me. 'Though Zac must be doing good things with her backhand. Did you know, she's four–one up in the deciding set?'

'[CHARLTON WORD],' bellowed Uncle Chris, before bashing the steering wheel again. '*Right then,*' he said.

What he did next surprised me. Instead of taking us back home – and letting me finish my Weetabix – he turned right, into Blackheath Village. He went straight across the roundabout and sped past the train station before overtaking a big line of cars at the pinch point by going on *completely the wrong side of the road.* Epic! After that he sped on, cutting in here, overtaking there, while all the time he shouted into his phone, which he'd shoved into a holder on the dashboard. In the first call he used the Charlton words loads, and some other words I'd never heard before but which sounded so bad they must have been Premier League words that you only hear at clubs like Arsenal or Chelsea. In the second he didn't speak at all. He just listened, going as pale as a sucked ice lolly as we went over London Bridge, after which he took some really big deep breaths. Two minutes later he jammed the car to a stop outside this massive glass building.

'It's take-your-nephew-to-work day.'

'Cool!'

'But we're not your nephews,' Billy objected.

'Then it's take your nephew and their pals to work.'

'And the people they hate,' Veronique added, while I just looked at Uncle Chris in shock.

'But I haven't cleaned my teeth,' I said.

Uncle Chris didn't seem to think that mattered because he jumped out of the car and told us to get a move on. I wanted to discuss enamel with him and bacteria, but I didn't get the chance – he stuck his phone to his head again and carried on shouting as he marched us through this big spinny door. We hurried through a huge foyer that was as echoey as the swimming pool, and then zoomed up in this really fast glass lift. All the while Uncle Chris shouted into his phone, and when the lift opened the man he was shouting at was on his phone shouting back at him. They did that for a second or two before shoving their phones in their pockets.

'We're shafted!' the other man shouted and Uncle Chris shouted,

'I can't believe this is [CHELSEA WORD], [ARSENAL WORD] happening!'

They carried on shouting and then rushed towards this enormous room with loads of people in. They were all wearing suits and sitting at desks and all of them were shouting too. I wanted to say what Mum says to me and Lance sometimes: *You're in the same room.* I didn't get a chance, though, because no one was paying attention to us. Uncle Chris seemed to have forgotten we were there until he spun round and saw us, after which he turned to the nearest desk, where a young woman was typing at a computer.

'What's your name?' Uncle Chris shouted.

'Shah, sir. Alisha.'

'And you are . . .?'

'Graduate trainee.'

'Well, today you're a graduate babysitter. You have to look after these three.'

'What?' the girl said.

'Buy them a hot chocolate or something. Or, if you like, tell them how a sudden crash in the global oil price coupled with record UK debt and a liquidity collapse means that, by 2 p.m., we are all probably going to be out of a [MAN CITY WORD] job!'

Uncle Chris pulled his wallet out and thrust a bundle of notes into the girl's hand, before running over to an office on the far side of the room.

The girl stared at the money and then at us, before Billy said, 'I don't like hot chocolate.'

I said, 'Have you got a toothbrush?'

'What's liquidity?' Veronique asked.

She found out over the next hour. We went out to some sofas near the lift and the young woman – Alisha – made a call. Five minutes later a load of food was delivered. There were croissants, chocolate croissants and swirly raisin things, as well as two hot chocolates and three orange juices. Billy and I tucked in and briefly I thought of Lance, who would have picked out the raisins because he hates them. I pushed any thought of HIM aside, though, and offered one to Veronique, though she wasn't interested. She really did want to know about liquidity, though Alisha wasn't sure about telling her.

'How old are you, sweetheart?'

'Nine.'

'Then I'm not really sure you'd –'

'*Try me*,' insisted Veronique.

Alisha did, as Billy and I stuffed ourselves, and I stared through the glass into the big room. The door was shut and no sound came out and the people waving their arms about looked like dying insects.

Meanwhile, Veronique was deep in conversation with Alisha, whose eyes were going wide as Veronique asked her questions.

'And how is LIBOR affected by a fiscal stimulus?'

'Er . . . that depends on the OBR.'

'Is that a football team?' I said.

Alisha didn't answer. Instead she went to fetch a flipchart, which she drew graphs on for Veronique. Billy and I had finished our croissants and were getting bored, so Billy got out his mobile phone (I *know* – in Year 4!). We played Minecraft and it felt weird because Veronique was right – I *hated* Billy. Or . . . did I? Being at the Tate with him had been okay. And it was okay now. He showed me some things I didn't know on Minecraft and agreed with my suggestions for a fort. I saw that his eye wasn't a purple or green eye now, but a light yellow one. I finally asked him how he got it, though instead of answering he squinted at me.

'You're lucky,' he said.

I felt anything but lucky right then. 'How?'

'You just are. I've always been jealous of you.'

'Of *me*?'

'Yeah.'

'Is that why you pick on me?'

Billy didn't answer. He just looked a bit ashamed and offered me the phone, but I didn't look down at it because Uncle Chris came flying in. Not to see us, though. He was shouting into his phone again and when the lift came up the person he was shouting at came out. Again they sort of carried on before putting their phones away and Uncle Chris stopped shouting. The other man, however, did not.

This man was older than Uncle Chris. He had a very red face and an enormous stomach. His shouting was so loud that when Billy glanced at me I knew what he was thinking: this guy's worse than Mrs Johnson.

'You've destroyed our entire firm!' he shouted, before shoving the door to the big room open. I thought Uncle Chris was going to follow but instead he just stood there in a daze. He stared at the door to the big room and I thought he would pull himself together and go in. But he didn't. Instead he began to sort of collapse on himself, slumping into a chair in front of us. And then we watched in pure amazement as, very carefully, he set his phone down on the floor in front of him and stamped it to bits with his heels.

Alisha gave a light gasp. We all stared at Uncle Chris with our eyes wide open. Nobody spoke until Veronique said, 'Were you selling short?'

Uncle Chris didn't answer, so I turned to Veronique.

'Selling *shorts*?'

'No. *Short*. Singular.'

'Right. Is that just one leg?'

'*Nooo*. Cymbeline, your Uncle Chris takes people's money and promises to buy parts of other people's companies with it. Okay?'

'If you say so.'

'These parts are called *shares*. When he does actually buy them he'll make money if the price has gone *down* since he promised. It's like hoping someone comes last on sports day.'

'So what's gone wrong then?'

'It doesn't work.'

'Like I've been trying to tell them,' Alisha said.

'Why not?'

'It's too risky. If the price goes up and not down you still have to buy them. And you lose money. You might be all right a few times but you're bound to be caught out, especially if your short positions are not predicted by general economic conditions. It's made worse if you post too much margin.'

What Veronique was on about I had NO idea, but I stared at the man opposite, who now had his head in his hands. Tears were streaming down his face.

'Did you post too much margin, Uncle Chris?'

'Yes.'

Uncle Chris stared up at me and nodded very slowly. He looked ashamed, like Gary Talbot when Miss Phillips asked him in front of the whole class if he'd taken Vi Delap's Match Attax out of her tray. Then he started crying even more and we all watched until Veronique did that hiss thing she does when she thinks people are being thick.

'So why don't you revert the short to a long position?'

'What?' said Alisha.

'Revert to long by flipping his investment model.'

'I've never heard that phrase.'

'I just made it up. But if he's been betting – wrongly – on who is going to lose at sports day, why not bet on the person you think will win? If share prices fall, a bold flip to a long stance on a percentage of the same stock should claw back most of his losses. Or have I got something wrong?'

'But my clients don't do that,' Uncle Chris said.

'Then you need to persuade them to or else they're going to lose their money, aren't they?'

'But how can I? My boss. He's hanging me out to dry.'

'You have to stand up to him, mate,' Billy said. 'Don't let him push you around.'

'But my reputation. I've been selling short. How can I push for reversion?'

'Here,' said Veronique, handing Uncle Chris some paper from the flipchart. 'I've drawn this out for you. Tell them to take long positions until you reach the percentage written there, and then you can go back to being evil, can't you?'

Veronique didn't get an answer to her question. Instead Uncle Chris just grabbed the paper, stared at it, and sprinted back into the big room. He left the door open and we heard shouting. *Louder* shouting. Shouting that sounded like *arguey* shouting. But then it sounded like *excited* shouting and after a while it sounded like *just-scored-a-goal-against-Rotherham* shouting and Uncle Chris came running back out.

'You beauties!' he shouted, before rushing back inside to more shouting.

It was good to see Uncle Chris happy again. Veronique got on with her croissants and we went back to Minecraft until Uncle Chris came out yet again (after more shouting). And he was grinning. He stared at Veronique before turning to look at Alisha.

'You're promoted.'

'To what?'

'My old job.'

'Your old . . .? What's your new job?'

'I'm the boss!' Uncle Chris shouted.

At that moment the older man with the red face who had shouted a lot at Uncle Chris came out with his tie hanging open. It was his turn to look like he was in a daze. He stared Uncle Chris in the face and then stumbled off towards the lift as loads more people from the big room came surging out, patting Uncle Chris on the back and asking him questions. Uncle Chris tried to calm them down, pushing them back into the big room, but before he went in himself he said, 'You guys. Tell Alisha what you want. Anything.'

Billy put his hand up. 'Ice cream?'

'Bucket-loads. Veronique?'

'Will she explain what 'securitisation' is?'

'Just ask her. Absolutely. And you, Cymbo?' Uncle Chris beamed, hanging on the doorframe. 'What can we get you, my super nephew?'

A thousand images flashed through my mind but there was only one thing I wanted.

'Can we go to Welling?' I said.

Alisha waved at a taxi outside the building and it stopped in front of us. It took quite a while to get to Welling, during which time she did tell Veronique what securitisation is (and, if you want to know yourself, ask *her*). When Veronique started asking questions, Alisha asked if she wanted to work in the City when she grew up.

'No way!' Veronique said, as the taxi pulled up at a red light.

Alisha looked offended. 'Oh. And why not?'

'Because an obsession with money drives you off the road to happiness.'

'Does it? And what is that?'

'Love, silly.'

'Yes. Of course. You do *need* money, though.'

'Agreed. And having a lot is okay. *If.*'

'If what?'

'It doesn't push you off the road to happiness.'

'Which is love. I see. But, well, how will I know if that's happening?'

'Easy, though most people don't know. Which is why they're unhappy. It's when the only people you find yourself loving, or even wanting to love, are people with a lot of money. Understand?'

Alisha did, so much so that after staring at Veronique for a second she pulled a notebook out of her bag and wrote that down.

'Can I come to see you sometimes? For a chat?'

Veronique said that would be fine, though with fencing, swimming, piano and language classes it would have to be on Saturday mornings. Before ten. Alisha wrote that down too.

Veronique and Alisha carried on chatting while I stared out of the window. When I saw the Greggs I directed the taxi driver down the side streets and he pulled up at the gates to the park. I was SO excited. I was here. Finally. I got out and started walking, Alisha asking what, exactly, we were doing.

'Do you live near here?'

'No,' I said.

'Is there a playground then or something?'

'No.'

'Well then, why have we –'

But I was too fired up to listen to any more. I ran right through the park, jumping up to press the buzzer on the heavy blue door.

CHAPTER NINETEEN

And this is what happened.

Almost immediately the door clicked. I pushed it open, not even waiting for Alisha and the others, just sprinting up to the desk and asking if I could see my mum.

'Janet Igloo,' I explained, when the woman looked confused. Why she was confused I didn't know because it was the same one as last time and she must have known who my mum was. I expected her to ask me to wait while she called the doctor, but she didn't. She just looked *even more* confused, until she said,

'But she's not here.'

'She's not . . .?'

'Here,' the woman said, reaching to pick up the phone as she stared at me.

CHAPTER TWENTY

At that moment Alisha hurried in with Veronique and Billy, wanting to know what was happening. Why were we here? The nurse was on the phone and so I told her. Everything just tumbled out – how I'd never been swimming and how Billy had challenged me to a race. How he'd pushed me in and how Mum had gone mad, then my waking up without Mum and coming to see her in here. Finding her paintings, not knowing what they meant. I even told her about Lance, and the Tate. Alisha went quiet as I spoke and so did Veronique, and Billy went quiet too. I was embarrassed at saying it all in front of him, but he didn't laugh. That was weird – were we friends now?

'And she's not here?' Alisha asked the nurse.

'She discharged herself,' the nurse replied. 'This morning.'

This was the second time that Mum had vanished, but it was completely different from the first time when I'd woken up with Uncle Bill there. That was terrible but this was the opposite – if she'd left the hospital it could only mean one thing: she was better! She was probably at our house, right now, wondering where I was! I grabbed Alisha's hand and tried to pull her out of the hospital, desperate to put everything I'd just told her behind me. Things could go back to the way they were *before*. Me and Mum, living together, being us. I didn't need to go swimming and I didn't care what her 'thing' about it was, as Veronique put it. I just wanted her back. But at that moment the tall doctor came out of the far door – Dr Mara.

'Cymbeline,' he said with his big deep voice. 'You're . . . here?'

'It's okay, I don't need the toilet. Mum's out now.'

'I know,' he said. 'It was before I came on shift. I would definitely have advised against that . . . But has she spoken to you? Has she told you anything?'

'No. I haven't spoken to her. We've been helping

my uncle keep his [CHELSEA WORD] job. I need to go and see her.'

'Right,' said Dr Mara, though he didn't sound too certain. 'When you do see her, you must ask her to give me a call. Please remember to do that, okay? "Call Dr Mara." It's extremely important. I've left messages for your Uncle Bill too but I haven't heard back from him. Please get him to call me as soon as possible.'

I didn't waste time explaining that Uncle Bill was away. I had to get out of there! I just said yes, I would, and then I dragged Alisha towards the exit. We got a taxi on the high street (after buying sausage rolls from the Greggs). We all piled in but Veronique said it wasn't fair: she'd been told what securitisation was and I'd got to go to Welling but Billy hadn't had his ice cream. Billy said it didn't matter, if we were going to see my mum. I thanked him, blushing a bit and thinking about Lance. Billy and I were . . . well, we were *friends* now, as weird as that sounds. I felt guilty for making judgements about him and it made me realise that the bit you actually see of a person is like the ears on the hippos on the Discovery Channel. There's much more underneath. This was true of Billy, and also of Lance. So if Billy was my friend now, was Lance going to be like Billy used to be? The answer was yes – after what he'd said about Mum I couldn't see any way I could be friends with him again, and he probably felt the same way after I'd punched him. I swallowed to think of how we'd be at school now, but I pushed that away because I was so psyched up about Mum, and when the taxi stopped on our street I leapt out as soon as the door clicked open.

'Mum!' I yelled, banging on the door. 'It's me! Mum!'

There was no answer. I sighed, wishing I had my bag with my keys. Was she asleep? She'd be tired, especially if she still had some of her headache. I banged on the door again but Alisha put her hand on my shoulder.

'She doesn't think you're here, does she?'

I blinked at her. 'What?'

'I mean, you wouldn't be living here on your own, would you? So I mean, where does she *think* you've been staying?'

I hadn't thought of that. 'Auntie Mill's!' I said.

The taxi was just turning round and Alisha managed to make it stop again. We got back in. I told the driver where to go, getting really annoyed at all the traffic near the new roundabout in Lewisham.

When we finally got past it I had this image. Mum would be in the big living room. I'd run round and she'd slide the glass door open, crouching down to my level, her arms opening out to me. I had a brief worry that she wouldn't be able to get in if Auntie Mill was still working on her backhand, but when we got there I saw Uncle Chris's car in the drive – which meant he was back. We all jumped out of the taxi – again – and I dodged round to the side of the house, stopping when I got to the big doors at the back.

I was so desperate to see Mum now, and not just to be with her. Her being away had made me realise things. Hard things. The biggest was that life wasn't quite as I'd always thought it was. All the things around me were, in some way, different. Mum, Auntie Mill, Juni and Clay, Lance and Billy. They were much more complicated than I'd ever known, made up of lots more ingredients than I'd thought, like when you look on the back of a cake and see the E numbers. And I didn't want them to be. I wanted things to be how they were, or at least for me to still see them like that, even if they weren't. Mum's being gone had torn this huge hole in the world around me and I'd been forced to look through it. I didn't want to look through it. I wanted Mum to stand in the way. I wanted to see her, not the world, and I wanted that more than anything.

But Mum didn't rush out to meet me. As I pulled the door open and stepped in I scoured the room to find her – but she wasn't there. I shook my head because where else could she be? Uncle Bill was away, so she can't have thought I'd be staying there. At the school perhaps? Trying to pick me up? No. She would have known it was an Inset Day. So was she buying my birthday present? If so, I didn't want her to be. As unbelievable as it might sound, I didn't care one bit about that. I didn't want anything, only her. I stood there thinking that of course Auntie Mill would know where she was. When Mum came out of the hospital she would have called her, wouldn't she? Even if they didn't get on that well, Mum would want to find me, and I was staying there.

But where was Auntie Mill? I couldn't see her. There was definitely something strange about that because she was *always* there. She was like the sofa or the TV; I'd *never* been there without her. And as I began to notice the room properly – not just Mum and Auntie Mill not being in it – I saw that the others were acting weird.

Juni and Clay were sitting at the table but they weren't arguing or on their phones as usual.

They were *crying*.

Juni was *really* crying and Clay was crying too. Alisha, Billy and Veronique arrived as I stared at Juni and Clay, almost unable to take that in. Then I turned to the other end of the room, where Uncle Chris had the phone in his hand. His jaw was trembling and his chest was heaving up and down, and I heard him say, 'Please. Just call me back. You have to call me *back*. Let's talk about this. Someone called *Zac*? I mean, are you serious? Really? Just call me back or, better still, come home. *Please* come *home*, Mill.'

CHAPTER TWENTY-ONE

The rest of that evening was terrible. After Uncle Chris hung up he immediately started to redial as I turned back to the table and saw what was on it. The envelope addressed to 'Chris' that Auntie Mill had put on the work surface that morning. It was open. Juni had the letter in her hand and I watched as she looked up from it, then tore it into pieces.

'She's left us,' Juni said, which made Clay cry even more.

Juni, Clay and Uncle Chris were so upset that it was sort of like I wasn't there. They were in their own bubble and I couldn't get through to them. Auntie Mill had *left*? How, 'left'? Mum had left, but she was ill. Had Auntie Mill just left on *purpose*? That was nearly impossible to understand. I did care that she'd left of course, but not as much as I wanted to know where *my* mum was. I couldn't ask anyone there for help, though. Uncle Chris kept calling Auntie Mill and then he called the tennis club, shouting at them because they wouldn't give him the phone number he wanted. Juni and Clay either hung around him, asking if he'd got hold of Auntie Mill yet, or they looked really dazed. All I could do was look out of the window, my last hope being that Mum had gone shopping for my present; she'd arrive any minute.

But when it got to eight o'clock I realised that the shops would have shut ages ago. I had no idea where she was and, even worse, I had no idea how to find her. Eventually I forced myself to tell Uncle Chris, who didn't understand what I was saying at first. But then he seemed to pull himself together. He called Auntie Mill – *again* – and when her voicemail came on he said, 'Please. We need to talk. We can work this out, but there's something more. Janet's walked out of the hospital and we don't know where she is. Has she called you? Please let us know – Cymbeline's frantic.'

I waited, really hoping that Auntie Mill would phone back. But she didn't. I wandered over to the window again and saw the flowers I'd bought for Mum that Auntie Mill had thought I'd got for her. They were in a vase on the windowsill, but the water they were standing in was brown and there were dirty rings going down the sides of the glass. The petals were dangling down from the stalks like hangnails and, as I watched, one of them dropped, rocking for a second on the sill before stopping.

Veronique and Billy had already gone home by then. But Alisha stayed and cooked some pasta with pesto for Juni, Clay and me, while Uncle Chris stayed on the phone. We couldn't eat much and afterwards Alisha got the Carcassonne out for a game, but Clay said he was going off to his room. I played but I kept looking out of the window for Mum. I didn't see her, but I did think Auntie Mill was back because I saw puffs of smoke coming from out of the treehouse. I told Uncle Chris and he ran down there and climbed the ladder. But it wasn't Auntie Mill.

'Clayton!' he bellowed. 'What on earth do you think you're doing? And, hey, what *is* that stuff?'

Alisha, Juni and I played Carcassonne while Uncle Chris took Clay up to his room to have a word with him. We played, without talking, until Veronique and her mum came in carrying dishes of food. Because we'd eaten, they put them in the fridge and then sat next to me. Seeing them together was weird. They looked so similar, like opening up a Russian doll to see the smaller one underneath. But I could also see Veronique's dad in her face too, probably because he's Chinese and Veronique's mum's not. It was so obvious that she was made up of two different, separate people. With only her mum next to her, it looked sort of like there was a bit of her missing. The bit of her that didn't come from her mum. It made me think about me. I was just made up of my mum. Her only.

She was all I had.

Veronique's mum put her arm round me and leaned down so that her face was really near. She smiled but it wasn't a pretending-everything-is-okay smile. It was more of a I-know-things-are-absolutely-terrible smile.

'Veronique told me about your mum,' she said. 'You don't know where she is, do you?'

There was nothing I could do but admit the truth. So I shook my head.

'And no one can get in touch with your aunt?'

'No. She's *really* working on her backhand. We can't reach Uncle Bill either because he's away.'

'And your mum wasn't at home when you went there?'

I saw myself banging on our door. 'No.'

'Have you tried calling home from here?'

'Uncle Chris has. There's no answer. I just don't know where she is.'

Veronique's mum shifted up right next to me and her arms went round my shoulder.

'I'm sure it'll be all right,' she said. 'She'll probably get here when you're asleep. But if she doesn't –'

'Yes?'

'Then I think we might have to call the police.'

CHAPTER TWENTY-TWO

I went to bed feeling numb. I picked up the tablet and stared at the black screen, trying to imagine Mum's face on it. But it stayed black. She wouldn't appear. I wanted to ask Uncle Chris if he had a charger but I didn't, not with everything else going on. I pushed it aside and lay on my back in the huge bed, wishing I could just be asleep so that I wouldn't have to feel what I was feeling. I wouldn't have to feel anything, nothing at all, though perhaps I might have a dream, which even if it was horrible couldn't be as bad as being awake. It might even be a good dream, with Mum in it, and for a second that thought lifted me. But actually I hoped I wouldn't dream about Mum, because waking up without her would be even worse then, wouldn't it?

Uncle Chris woke me up the next morning. He was wearing the same suit as yesterday, which made him smell of yesterday and everything that had happened then. Just seeing him, the look on his face, told me that Mum hadn't got there during the night. I followed him downstairs and saw Veronique and her mum back in the living room again, smiling up at me from the sofa. A policewoman was standing next to them.

I stared at the policewoman, slowly, reluctantly remembering why she was there.

Veronique's mum stood up. 'Cymbeline, this is Sergeant Cartwright.'

'Catherine,' the policewoman said.

She asked me to sit down, which I did. Everyone was watching me and a strange, still atmosphere spread around as Catherine perched next to me on the sofa.

I was hot, and uncomfortable, and barely able to speak when she smiled and asked me what had been 'going on'. I got the words out, though, going through it all as I'd done with Alisha the day before, even the bit about going back to my house at night. And what I'd found there.

'She only *ever* painted Mr Fluffy,' I said.

'I see.' Catherine scribbled that down on a pad and looked up at me. 'I think. Mr . . .?'

I told her all about Mr Fluffy and then about Not Mr Fluffy (But Teddy In His Own Right). I asked if she wanted to see him but Catherine said no, though she would like to see my painting. I fetched it and Catherine studied it for a minute before telling me it was really good and reaching forward to take a photo of it on her phone. Her sleeve rode up when she did that and a snake poked its head out before ducking back in again. I didn't know police people were allowed to have tattoos and I wondered if she had a whole jungle, lions and tigers and elephants all running around underneath her stiff black clothes.

Catherine asked what Mum's height was and Uncle Chris had to answer because who knows that about their own mum? She said she was sure Mum was going to turn up and she smiled again, which got me really frustrated. She wasn't making calls. She wasn't sending out copies of the picture. She seemed far too relaxed about Mum being missing. I couldn't describe *how absolutely wrong* it was that Mum hadn't come to find me after leaving the hospital. Was she still ill? Had she *tried* to find me but couldn't for some reason? That thought made me want to cry and Catherine put her hand on my arm.

'I'm sure she'll turn up, love. Really. Meanwhile I'll ask my colleagues to keep an eye out for her.'

'But you don't understand. She should be *here*. She really should be. Especially today.'

'Today?'

'Because it's my birthday,' I said.

That comment seemed to change the atmosphere. Veronique's mum's mouth opened but she shut it, quickly, her hand going up to her mouth as she studied me. Catherine looked more serious. She stood, thanking me quickly before asking Uncle Chris to show her out.

I watched them chatting on the front doorstep before she left, then Catherine started speaking into her walkie-talkie before Uncle Chris had even closed the door. Meanwhile Veronique's mum was squeezing my shoulder, her head cocked to one side, and her eyes were a bit shiny. I gave her a quick smile and looked around at the room, amazed because it was only when I'd said it that I remembered what day it was. It was so weird. All the anticipation, like water pressing up to a dam, and I'd just forgotten. I normally wake up buzzing, almost unable to believe that the day has actually come. And this one was going to be an even better birthday than normal because, for the first time that I could remember, it was on a Saturday. A WEEKEND. For weeks I'd been imagining waking up at home, with Mum, early, knowing I didn't have to rush about, that I could just jump into her bed with her and open my presents and watch *The Simpsons* on her tablet. Seeing it in my mind's eye at that moment, it was almost as if it really was happening – but to a different Cymbeline. Not me. A Cymbeline living the life that should have been mine. I wanted to run home again. I wanted to make the imagined birthday true, but I couldn't of course. I was the Cymbeline in this Cymbeline's life and there was nothing I could do about it.

Veronique's mum coughed and then wished me happy birthday before asking what I wanted to do. I shrugged.

'Well, what do you normally do on a Saturday?'

'He plays football,' Veronique said.

I frowned at Veronique, wondering how she knew this, though it was obvious, actually. On Mondays we do go on about it, replaying our goals or complaining that Danny Jones has to pass it more. Everyone knows

200

about Saturday football and I'd been looking forward to it because on my birthday Mr Delap (Vi's dad/our coach) wouldn't make me go in goal *at all*. That didn't matter now, though, and when Veronique's mum asked if I wanted to go today, I said no because I wanted to wait here for my mum.

'But if you normally go, that's where she'll think you'll be, won't she?'

I hadn't thought of that so I agreed, and Veronique's mum asked if Veronique wanted to go as well.

'But what about Mandarin? And French? *And* piano?'

'You can catch up later. During reading time. Yes?'

'Football,' said Veronique. 'Hmmm.'

Uncle Chris drove us. Clay lent me some old boots and shorts and Veronique and I got into Uncle Chris's car. Billy came round for a lift as well. I was pleased to see him, which you are with a friend, and that finally proved that he *was* my friend, though the first thing he did was ask me if my mum had come back. That hurt, and it didn't get any better when I remembered that Mum normally drops me off at football. We do drills and stuff and then Mum comes back to watch the match at the end – *with the other parents*. They'd ask me where she was and I'd have to say I didn't know. I shivered when I thought of all the kids in my team asking too, which they would because I'd told them Mum was going to bring cakes because of my birthday. And then I shivered even more because of course one of those kids would be my supposed best friend, who'd said my mum was crazy.

Lance – sorry, I mean Bradley – *had been* going to come back to my house after football. Mum *had been* going to take us to see a film. She'd promised us popcorn, and not homemade stuff in old Iceland bags but bought in the *actual cinema* (without Mum even tutting about how expensive it was). This was my special outing. It wasn't going to happen of course, but I was still going to have to see him. Was he going to laugh? Would he have some great joke up his sleeve about Mum being missing? I felt sick at that thought and when Uncle Chris pulled up by the heath I wanted to stay in the car.

He wasn't there yet, though, so when Billy and Veronique scrambled out I grabbed my bag and followed them on to the grass. Uncle Chris said he'd pick us up later and drove away, and Billy ran off towards Danny.

I looked for Mum, squinting against the sun, my hand shading my eyes as I scanned the huge green space all the way up to the road near Greenwich Park, where the cars looked like they were being pulled by a piece of string. There were so many people, near or far away, but I didn't have to look at each one to know Mum wasn't there. She felt not there.

I just shook my head and then looked at the coach-dads putting poles out and the kids getting ready to play, some kicking balls, others shouting, some in school kits but others in their own shirts with Messi on the back or Ronaldo or Sturridge, though Mickey in Year 5 had some random person because he supports Grimsby Town. Without Mum it didn't look real. It felt as if I wasn't actually there, not in the wrong Cymbeline's life any more, but in no life. A ghost. Vi Delap and her brother Franklin (Year 6) were trying to do headers while their little sister Frieda (Reception) grabbed hold of Franklin's legs. I could hear them laughing, but it was like they were a thousand miles away, or on telly

When Franklin kicked the ball towards me I stared at it, hardly knowing what to do, though usually I'd have been nervous because he's older, and really good, and

I wouldn't have wanted it to go under my foot. I would have trapped it and chipped it back, or even done a rabona to impress him. But I just watched it bang up against my leg before nudging it to Veronique.

She looked a little confused. 'Kick it,' I said.

'Oh.'

She did, trying to toe-prod it, though she got the edge and it spun off towards the Year 2s. I went to get it and I kicked it back to Franklin, who was on his own now because Vi was digging in her bag. She ran up and I thought she was going to be the first to ask where my mum was, and I steeled myself for that. But instead she held out something to me.

A birthday present.

I was relieved. But I also felt guilty. Vi had got me a present and I hadn't invited her to see *Star Wars*. The present also made me feel strange because, again, I couldn't connect to it. It didn't mean anything, which made me realise that actually presents never do. Birthdays aren't about them, but about being in your family, right at the very middle of it, all of it moving around you for one whole day. Nothing else mattered without that.

And maybe that was why nothing seemed real to

me – because without Mum there was nothing for me to be in the middle of.

I said thanks, though. It was really nice of her. I smiled, about to take the present, but I didn't. Because I couldn't. And *that* was because, weirdly – and I do *mean weirdly* – Veronique leapt forward and grabbed it out of Vi's hand!

I stared, confused, my first impulse being to shout 'Hey!' and grab it back. But Veronique had been really nice to me in the last few days, and I also knew that she had problems of her own. She was always *doing* things. She did more things than I even knew there were *to* do. It must be exhausting. Was this some reaction? Was she going a bit mad, nicking people's birthday presents? Instead of complaining, I smiled and was about to hold out my hands so Veronique could give me the present back. But before I could do that she did something even more weird – she started to unwrap it. And not just unwrap, but tear and rip, scrabbling at the paper like a two-year-old until the actual present fell on to the grass.

That really was a bit much and I was about to reach down and pick it up when Veronique suddenly shoved the paper in my face.

'Look!' she insisted.

'Yes. It's *quite* nice to take it off yourself , you know.'

'I *know*. But don't you *see*?'

'Yes,' I said, pushing Veronique's hand away from my nose. 'Reindeers.'

'It was all we had in,' Vi said. 'You don't mind, do you?'

'Of course not. And thanks for –'

'DON'T YOU SEE?' shouted Veronique.

I didn't, but Veronique's behaviour was so weird that instead of bending down to the present I watched her as she spread her hands out, shouted again, and then dropped down to her knees – to my bag. Not asking me if she could, she pulled the zip and started yanking things out of it. Eventually she came out with the picture of Mr Fluffy and spread it out on the grass. I was cross – she was being rough with it, and it *was* mine – but I couldn't help following her finger as she jabbed it down on the picnic rug. No, not the rug – the balled-up pieces of paper on it.

And I *could* see.

Wrapping paper.

It wasn't litter. It wasn't paper for sandwiches. It was obvious now.

Mum had painted *wrapping paper*. Which meant . . .

My mouth fell open. Vi asked what was going on but we both just glued our eyes to the picture and ignored her (sorry, Vi). I stared at Veronique's finger on the paper, then followed it as it moved – to Mr Fluffy.

'It's for him,' she said.

'For . . .?'

'It's for *Mr Fluffy*. It's for *him*. He was in it. You had just been given him. In the painting. He was wrapped up. And that means that in the picture –'

'It's my birthday,' I said.

CHAPTER TWENTY-THREE

We were silent for a second. Then Veronique said something that was really obvious but still needed saying.

'And it's your birthday today. It's your birthday today as well, Cymbeline.'

'What's going *on*?' Vi said.

Again we ignored her. We weren't being rude. We were just too stunned, and having the same thought. The picture scene was on my birthday – that was now clear. But that wasn't all: we also knew the time. Veronique had worked that out from the shadows.

Midday.

It was only two hours from now.

And if Mum wasn't here, where she knew I'd be, or at home, *or* at Auntie Mill's, where else could she be?

She had to be *there*, where the picture was, and she had to be there *right now*. Or at least she would be soon. She'd painted the same painting, of the same day, at the same time, over and over again.

And we still had no idea where it was.

But then Vi bent down to my present. I turned from the picture to see her holding it out to me: a Charlton shirt. She'd got me one, something so kind and great that for a second it drew me away from the painting. A home shirt, a proper one, which I know is really expensive. And not only that. She turned it over and I saw that she'd got my name done on the back. I couldn't help but smile, imagining wearing it, though the smile turned to excitement. My name.

Of course.

I still hadn't finished the picture of Mr Fluffy, had I? It was my turn to drop down to my knees and scrabble in my bag. I grabbed a pencil and wrote the words that Mum had painted and which I'd forgotten to put on Mr Fluffy's T-shirt. They were 'Eglinhs Hretigae'.

'Oh, *Cymbeline*,' said Veronique. 'Your spelling is *terrible*!'

CHAPTER TWENTY-FOUR

And here's what happened next. Vi's dad called her over to put her boots on and she ran off. Veronique sounded like a kettle about to boil as she explained that it was not 'Eglinhs Hretigae'; it was *English Heritage*. She told me that it was this organisation that looks after castles and big houses, though I already knew that. We'd been to one on Clay's birthday once, where the Cavaliers were supposed to attack the Roundheads, but the Roundheads' minibus had been stuck in traffic. When they did finally show up, they must have been in a hurry because one of them was still eating a Mars bar and this other one, who died right in front of us, had left his phone on. Someone rang him and it played 'I'm Forever Blowing Bubbles' from inside his gunpowder pouch as he went red. Clay had started to boo.

'I'm glad you're dead,' he said. 'I hate West Ham.'

A man in the crowd behind us leaned forward and told him to '*Watch it*'.

English Heritage. On Mr Fluffy's T-shirt. It was an English Heritage place that Mum had painted. That's where he'd come from.

'But how do we know which *one*?' I said.

'Billy's phone!' squealed Veronique, before running off to find him.

Billy ran back with her and we watched, hardly able to breathe, as he went into Google (on his phone, in Year 4, I know!). I'd been to one English Heritage place and Veronique said she'd been to two at least. That was three, but did they have any more than that?

'Four hundred,' Billy said.

'*What?*'

'Says here, "English Heritage looks after four hundred of England's historic buildings."'

'So which one is it?' I cried, once again staring down at the picture.

And that was it. The end. It had to be. What else could we do? We had less than *two hours* if we wanted to get there by midday. And they had *four hundred places.* I turned to Veronique, knowing that she was a brilliant, everything-speaking Grade Five genius. But she had no answer. And Billy just shrugged. For the last time I squinted at the painting, my eyes boring into the paint. And I was so frustrated, almost as if it was teasing me on purpose, giving little pieces of meaningless help but never the one thing that mattered. On impulse I snatched it up from the grass, about to tear it into pieces, when Billy grabbed my hand.

'There must be something,' he said. 'Some way of knowing which one it is.'

'But what? How can we *tell*?'

'Easy,' said a voice right behind me.

And it was him. Lan . . . Bradley. I hadn't seen him arrive. I spun round and there he was, in his St Saviour's kit. I folded my arms, about to tell him to *get lost*. But Veronique leapt forward.

'Easy?'

'Course.'

'So you mean . . .' She could hardly bring herself to say it. 'You know where this place is?'

'Course,' said Bradley again, and he pointed to the top of the painting, at all the people walking past.

Or on bikes.

'Whitecross House. I go there all the time.'

'You . . .?'

'With me and my dad's cycling club.'

'Your . . .?'

'My *dad*-dad,' he added. 'Why do you want to know?'

I told Bradley what had happened, and *begged* him to tell me where Whitecross House was.

'Depends,' he said.

'On what?'

'Well, are we friends again, or aren't we?'

'YOU ARE!' yelled Billy and Veronique.

CHAPTER TWENTY-FIVE

Five minutes later we were in Bradley's dad-dad's car. He'd dropped Bradley off and had been loping down into the village to get a coffee when we ran after him and stopped him. Veronique explained as quickly as possible what had happened because I just couldn't say it again. We all *pleaded* with him to take us to Whitecross House. But he shook his head. Then he scratched the back of it, saying he should call my uncle first, and Billy and Veronique's parents too.

'But that'll take too long! And I don't have Uncle Chris's number.'

'Be that as it may. I can't drive a bunch of kids around the countryside without their parents' say-so. You'll just have to –'

'But that's what *he'd* say,' Bradley said, grabbing his dad-dad's arm.

'Who?' said his dad-dad.

'Derek,' Bradley insisted. '*He'd* be safe and boring. *He* wouldn't help at all. Saying no, that's what *he'd* do.'

His dad-dad's back straightened. 'Come on then!' he said.

His car was parked back near the school and we all piled in, pushing aside cycling magazines and old water bottles. His dad-dad drove on to the main road and then down past the running track we do our sports days on. We went past GOALS where David Finch had had his last birthday party and Marcus Breen threw up on him, and after that I didn't recognise where we were. There was traffic and then bigger roads and then a turn-off on to smaller ones. I kept looking at the time on Billy's phone and Bradley saw me wincing.

'Come *on*, Dad!'

'I'm going as fast as I can, son. There's a speed limit, or didn't you know?'

'Of course I do but . . .'

'Three points you know, even for just a few miles over. It would put the insurance way up.'

'I *know*, Dad. But you should see *him* drive.'

'Him?'

'Derek. Blimey. Mum says he's just like Lewis Hamilton.'

'*Is* he now?'

His dad-dad put his foot down and the car lurched forward. He overtook a tractor but had to slow down after that. But it wasn't his fault. A queue of cars stretched ahead of us, the end ones turning left into some gates where a man in a bright green jacket was waving them through.

'This is it!' yelled Bradley, and I glanced at Billy's phone again. I screwed my hands into fists while the cars crawled along, impatience swarming inside me like wasps.

'Wait!' bellowed Bradley's dad-dad, as I threw the back door open.

I pretended not to hear and sprinted up towards the gate. The others all followed. All four of us darted past the man and into a huge grass car park where other people in green jackets were telling the cars where to go.

We ran past them and up to a wooden hut with people paying. Billy sprinted past and the people in the hut didn't blink, assuming he had a family up ahead. I followed him, but the sight of a huge house stopped me for a moment. Massive steps led up to a stone terrace and big chimneys shot out of the roof like rocket boosters.

Veronique grabbed hold of my arm. '*Look*,' she shouted, spinning me round to the right.

There were gardens, ordered and neat, surrounded by a low wall, and I thought that was what she meant. But beyond them was a field, sloping down to some trees, the land rising above them towards hills, where huge clouds marched forward. I stared but my eyes were drawn down to the trees again, and through them. For there was something glinting, shining, something sparkling through the trees like it was alive, a giant snake perhaps, slithering along in the valley. My mouth went dry and my feet stood still until Veronique pulled me forward alongside the little wall and into a field where the first thing I saw was a young woman reaching down to pick buttercups out of the grass. And then I stopped when I saw the picnic rug.

For a second I couldn't move. It wasn't that I knew the people sitting on the rug – I didn't – but because it was like I was in the painting. I was *in* it. I was standing in my own painting. These people had a pushchair too, a baby crawling around on the grass.

'Cymbeline!' Veronique called out.

She'd gone on and I followed towards the trees and then through them, dazzled by what was in front of me. It was wide, and swirling, with jagged edges like a cheese grater. The surface seemed to burn until the sun was snaffled by a cloud. Then I was on the bank and right near me the water was slow and deliberate, shifting in different directions like it was made of black glass plates. But in the middle of the river the water was angry and snarling, carrying off branches and bits of wood, moving faster than some runners on the far bank. And this was it. The missing centre of the picture – what Mum left out, what she couldn't paint – and thinking of her seemed to conjure her up, right there in front of my eyes.

Because she *was* there. Actually there. She was right there in in front of me.

In the river.

Veronique's hand went up to her mouth. Just like her mum's had earlier. Mum was to our right. She was standing up to her waist in the river, and the first thing I saw was that she was in her clothes. Not a swimming costume. Deciding to swim was mad enough, surely, but in her jeans and jumper?

'Mum! Mum!!'

But the water was too loud. She couldn't hear me. I waved my arms and screamed again, turning to see Bradley, who'd caught up and spotted Mum. Shouting out that he'd get his dad, he sprinted back, as Veronique started to pull her shoes off. Billy did the same thing and I watched, helpless, as they both waded out into the slow bit of the water, knowing I couldn't follow them.

When they were deep enough they launched themselves forward, Veronique darting ahead until she got to the place where the water was moving more quickly. Billy caught her up and they both fought to go forward, towards Mum, into the fast bit, but the water was too quick, too strong, it pushed them back the way they'd come before moving them down, level with me and then past, both of them swept back into the bank.

I ran round and grabbed Billy first, and then Veronique, both soaking, dragging them out on to the grass as I felt something. A silent shout. A pull that wasn't physical but real nonetheless, and meant for me alone. And when I obeyed it, and looked back out across the river, Mum was staring at me.

It's hard to describe how it felt. I stared back across the water, our eyes seeming to lock tight, Mum very far away from me but so close too, as close as I've ever been to her. I mouthed her name and saw her wince, her lips trembling as she looked at me, not noticing the water behind her, which seemed somehow to gather, and then surge. And Mum stumbled.

She didn't mean to. She just stumbled, to the side first before spinning and falling backwards, into the angry middle of the river.

'Mum!'

But she was in the water. She couldn't hear me. Her arms were flailing, the river seeming gleeful, snatching her like a ball and carrying her off. I moved, jogging along the bank, mirroring Mum. Billy and Veronique came after me. Mum was moving faster now so I started to run, trying to keep level with her. The people having the picnic stood up, probably because of all the shouting. And Bradley was shouting too, though he wasn't with his dad. I thought he was on his own but he wasn't, he was running alongside a car. A big car driving right through the middle of the field towards me.

'I saw it in the car park,' Bradley shouted. 'Your aunt was getting out. I told her about your mum and –'

I didn't hear what else Bradley had to say, turning my attention to Auntie Mill instead, expecting her to jump out, to dive in the river too. But she didn't. After a quick glance at me she gunned the engine forward, past me, heading straight towards the river bank, and don't talk to me about gas guzzlers or planet killers because Auntie Mill's car is epic. It took her over the bank and into the middle of the river, quite a way downstream of Mum, who ploughed straight into the side of the car where Auntie Mill was. Auntie Mill reached out of her window to grab hold of her.

And she *did* grab hold of her.

Auntie Mill grabbed Mum's hair and her arm and Mum held on. Auntie Mill pulled her towards her window and she would have got her through. I know it. She would have saved her for certain. Mum's head was almost through when it happened. Mum was holding on to Auntie Mill. They were both crying in the middle of the river and I could just hear them over the sound of the water – until the creak. It was a wrenching, horrible sound, coming from the car, which was side-on to the river. In disbelief I watched as slowly the river turned the car, twisting it backwards until Auntie Mill was unable to hold on to Mum, who was flung back into the water again and spun away from me.

So all I could do was watch. Mum scrabbled backwards, grabbing at the doorframe, catching the wing mirror for a second before she lost her hold. And then she tumbled away, sometimes above the water, her red jumper flashing, then below it. Her face came up, all white, and when she went under again I thought the river had taken her forever.

Until I saw the man.

He was at a bend in the river, right on the edge of the bank, getting ready. He was crouching, so I couldn't really see him, just his jeans and his shirt and black hair. Someone from the picnic? I didn't think so. Was it Uncle Bill? Had he come back? Yes! I started to run as he leapt into the water – towards Mum – and grabbed her, wrestling her round, fighting the river for her until he pulled her over to the side.

There was a little hill. I had to get over it. And there was Mum on the grass, all wet and shaking, clinging on to the man, and I so wanted to leap down into her arms. But the man turned. He turned away from Mum and stared at me, right into my face, and that was the first time ever that I saw my dad.

CHAPTER TWENTY-SIX

My dead-dad.

CHAPTER TWENTY-SEVEN

Here's something you won't believe. I, Cymbeline Igloo, have been swimming.

I have been swimming exactly fourteen times.

Well, maybe not swimming exactly, all those times. I did a lot of *standing* at first and then a lot of *holding on* to these long things called noodles. I did it at Lewisham Pool, which brought everything back at first (being pushed in, going under, Mum coming, etc., etc.). After a few times it was okay, though, and it was okay again today, but I won't tell you about today just yet. I'll leave that until last because you probably want to know about my dad first, don't you? I don't blame you, so I'll explain that, though you are *so going to love* what Marcus Breen did at the swimming pool today.

Do grown-ups tell you stuff? The real stuff that's bad sometimes, really bad maybe, all the stuff that happens in life? Real life? Do they tell you the actual truth, or do they try to shove it to one side like an old tent stuffed behind the sofa? Maybe they just tell you some of it. They paint a picture you can live in, a copy of real life, but with stuff left out. This was what the adults were discussing – Mum and Auntie Mill, Uncles Bill and Chris, and my dad of course – while I was supposed to be down in the treehouse with Clay and Juni. I was standing at the door, though, listening, and I knew what the answer was.

They shouldn't leave things out. They just shouldn't. They have to paint it all, the whole thing, and they shouldn't be afraid of that. If they hold us tight enough, so tight we know they love us, it won't matter what they say. Their love will get us through it. They couldn't see that, though, and were arguing, so I walked right in there and told them. They went quiet, and stared at me, until Auntie Mill did a hard sigh, about to snap *go off and play*. But instead she opened her mouth and started to nod, and Uncle Chris put his hand on her shoulder.

'Why don't you sit down?' he said to me.

And I did.

Uncle Chris was sitting forward on the sofa, not wearing a suit today but a blue shirt and cream trousers with creases down the front. Auntie Mill was next to him wearing normal things and then came Uncle Bill, who didn't look normal because he'd shaved his beard off. His face was a bit embarrassing to look at, like it didn't have any clothes on. Mum was in a chair, in a sweatshirt of Auntie Mill's, and my dad was sitting on the floor beside her, looking, well, just – sorry, Dad – *wrong*. I still couldn't quite take it in that he'd come down from the mantelpiece. Into the world. He made everywhere look a bit crowded.

'Right,' said Uncle Chris. 'Are you ready, Cym?'

'Yes,' I said, which was a fib, because I was a very lot not ready, and I'd like to apologise for that.

Uncle Chris put his elbows on his knees and took a big breath through his nose. Everyone stared at him, wondering what he'd say, and that was weird because of course they all *knew* what he was going to say. Maybe they just wanted to know where he'd begin. They didn't have to wait long.

'Your aunt used to be an actress,' he said and Auntie Mill sighed.

'I called myself an *actor*.'

'I know,' I said. 'She told me. And when she was doing Shakespeare Mum stole Dad off her. Didn't you, Mum?'

Mum's eyes opened in shock, and I thought she was going to cry, but Auntie Mill squeezed her knee and turned to me.

'No,' she said. 'I may have told you that, Cymbeline, but it's not true. He just preferred her. That's all. He didn't owe me anything and he had every right to –' she glanced at my dad and then looked away – 'and she couldn't help liking him. It wasn't your mum's fault. In fact, it was . . .'

'Yes, Auntie Mill?'

'Well, it was something I should have accepted. I should have accepted it but . . .'

'You didn't,' said Uncle Chris.

There was silence then as Auntie Mill swallowed. Accepted? I tried to work out what she meant.

'And is that why you argue?'

'Yes. That's it really.'

'But what's it got to do with Mr Fluffy and the painting?'

'Well,' Auntie Mill said, 'when you were born it got

worse if anything. I was really jealous. On your first birthday your mum invited me on an outing. So that we could be friends again. We always used to go to this place when we were kids.'

'Whitecross House?'

'Yes. And your mum wanted to take you there. And we went and at first it was fine.'

'It was lovely,' my dad said. 'Perfect. We looked round the house. We bought you a present from the shop.'

'Mr Fluffy?'

'And then we sat down by the river.'

'On the checked rug?'

'Yes.'

'At midday?'

'Yes, Cym.'

'And did you go and buy coffee?'

My dad glanced at my mum then, but she looked at Auntie Mill, who swallowed again. Then she said, 'Well, that's just it. Your mum went. She offered to go to the café and get them.'

'That was nice of her.'

'Yes, it was. But when she came back she hadn't brought me any sugar.'

'You have two sugars.'

'Yes. I do. And it was such a small, small thing and I was so silly. I . . . Well, I complained. I said she never really thought about me, about what I wanted. Such a tiny thing, but we started to argue and it grew, and then it all came out – how I resented her, how she got everything she wanted and I didn't. We really argued and the other people there were all watching so we stormed off and carried on in the car park. Arguing. And, well, that meant we left you . . .'

'With me,' my dad said.

He looked up at me then, and I squinted into his face. It really was weird to see him in the flesh. I knew he was my dad because of his photograph, but I didn't know how to feel. I'd never had a dad, had I, and it wasn't like what I felt with Mum, the feeling just coming straight out of me. I knew then that it was something I'd have to learn, like Bradley did with his new-dad. I wondered if my dad would have to learn it about me too.

'Cymbeline,' he said. 'I'm sorry.'

'That you're not dead?'

'No. About what I've got to tell you. No matter what anyone says, it was *my* fault. And only mine.

All of it. Your mum and your aunt went off and I knew what I had to do. I had to watch you. It shouldn't have been hard and it wasn't hard. You were crying because of the shouting, I think, and I calmed you down. I played with you. But then . . . Oh Lord.' My dad stopped speaking and squeezed his eyes shut, as if trying desperately not to see something.

'Yes?'

'Well, there was this job. A part in a TV thing. I'd had an audition that had gone really well and I was close to getting it, I knew I was. And, just at that moment, the director phoned me. I thought he was calling to say I'd got it. But he wasn't quite. He wanted to know stuff. This and that, all sorts of things. I had to convince him. And while I talked to him I put you down.'

'On the rug?'

'Yes. On the rug. And I was on the phone and the guy was going on and on, and I just, I just, I wasn't paying attention, Cym. I didn't notice. I took my eye off you. Not for long. A minute. And . . . you crawled away.'

'Babies can crawl, yes. Not swimming crawl obviously. But from between eight and twelve months they can do it, *and* pull themselves upright.'

'Well, you did.'

'And I crawled towards the river?'

Dad stared at me. When he answered his voice was almost silent. 'Yes.'

'And fell into it?'

'No,' my dad said.

I frowned. '*No?*'

'No,' he repeated, and there was another silence, even deeper than the others had been, everyone completely still, like the flowers in the garden are in the evening sometimes. They stared at me. And I stared back. I was *sure* I'd gone in the river. Wouldn't that explain *everything*? Not being allowed to go swimming, Mum going mad at the pool, going to that place on my birthday? If I *hadn't* fallen in the river, then what was it *all about*? I looked from face to face, each like a statue, until Mum's cracked into tears: which is when I knew. When I guessed. The very last thing the painting had to tell me.

The *two* balls of screwed-up wrapping paper.

And the baby clothes Mum didn't sell on eBay.

The photos that I'd *thought* were of me and Bradley.

'Your brother did,' Mum said.

CHAPTER TWENTY-EIGHT

I walked right up to the edge of the pool and curled my toes over. Today. I took a big deep breath, the air tangy, though not weird because I was used to it now. The water in front of me was all blue, and shimmering, and deep, and the other end seemed sooooooooo faaaaaaar away. A length. A WHOLE length. Could I do it? Really get there? I swallowed, then pulled my goggles down over my eyes and did a big stretch, like I'd seen Billy do in his race, which he'd won by about three miles. He was sitting on the side with Bradley and Veronique, who all gave me these big thumbs-up and grinned, which only made my legs feel even weaker than they already did. I turned back and looked along the line at the other kids, from all the other schools, getting ready as the man in the red shirt said, 'On your marks . . .' I blinked and turned forward, though immediately I looked behind me at the seating where all the parents were. Lance's dad-dad waved. Veronique's mum waved too, before putting that hand up to her mouth, the other on the sleeve of the woman next to her.

Mum.

My poor mum. She was staring at me, her eyes wide open, both of her hands out in front of her in fists. Her mouth was clamped shut and it didn't look like she'd taken a single breath for hours. I realised then that, as nervous as I was, it was *so much worse* for her. Watching me about to go into the water must have been dreadful. It was so brave of her to come, and I wanted to rush over and hug her and tell her that I was going to be okay.

But I didn't get a chance.

'GO!' the man shouted.

Water. It *can* hurt and I thought it was going to then, but it didn't. Much. I tried to dive like Veronique had in her race (which she'd also massacred), all dipping and smooth, and though I didn't quite do that, I did manage to stay away from the bottom.

And then I moved forward, my head down, my arms like windmills, the sound all thuddy and intense until, yes, it grew a bit calmer and more even, because I was doing it, I WAS SWIMMING, and it felt so thrilling and easy, and not just in a physical way, but also in my head, as if I was leaving behind the boy who'd been standing on the edge just seconds ago worrying about his mum. And in a sense I was leaving him, though I'd been doing that every day, it seemed, ever since Dad had told me what had happened.

I didn't speak for a second. I just stared at Dad as he stared back and then reached into the pocket of his jeans. He pulled his wallet out and from that drew a small, creased photo of two babies. Without speaking he touched his finger to one and I blinked at its wide open face, smiling up at me. Suddenly I felt very small.

'What was his name?' I said.

'Antony,' he croaked, and I nodded.

'Like, "And Cleopatra"?'

'Yes. That's right. Antony. He just . . .'

Dad couldn't speak after that and I knew why. They didn't have to tell me what happened. I looked down at my lap and rolled the name around in my brain.

'Antony,' I said, and it felt weird, as if they were telling me he had just been born, which he had in a way. In my head. Put there for the first time. But it shouldn't have been the first time, should it?

'Why did no one tell me?' I said.

The adults all looked at each other then. And then they started to argue again, reasons coming, excuses and apologies and more tears, and it sort of washed over me because I knew what the answer was. I was a little baby, then a child. They didn't want to paint the real picture. They thought they could paint one that would be easier for me to live in, without realising that you can't live if you don't live in the real painting. In the truth. I left them there, arguing, and went back down to Juni and Clay in the treehouse. We'd done the outside blue with a green roof, and on the inside we had a wall each to do pictures of ourselves on. Clay had painted himself as a lead guitarist with skulls all around him. Juni had done herself fencing. I'd done myself in my St Saviour's kit, holding a football, but I painted over that.

'What are you doing?' Juni asked, but I didn't answer. I just painted a little baby in my arms instead.

We went home then. The three of us: Mum and me, and Dad. Walking in felt weird, and even more so to have Dad there. In our house. Where Mum and I live. Mum turned the heating on and then the lights, apologising for not having any proper food in. We had pizza from Iceland, which was great, and then Mum came up with me to put my pyjamas on. I could hear Dad downstairs and so I whispered my next question.

'Why did you tell me he was dead?'

Mum shuddered. 'It was so horrible, Cym. After what happened. I couldn't even look at him. I didn't want to see him ever again.'

'But why did you tell me he was *dead*?'

'Because I told him to go away and never come back. And I thought it would be easier for you that way.'

'But why did he agree? He's my dad.'

'Because he felt so guilty about what happened. And because he was terrified he'd let something like that happen to you as well. But the real reason is because we were stupid,' Mum said. 'We all were. We were all so very stupid, Cym.'

I thought about that and then asked what she'd been doing in the river.

Mum stared at me and took a deep breath. 'I just wanted to be close to him,' she said. 'To Antony. The last place that he was.'

I wanted to know more, but there was no point, not then. I just concentrated on how great it was to have Mum back, telling her everything I'd done to work things out and find her.

'You won't ever have to do that again,' Mum said, before interfering with my hair.

Dad asked if he could stay that night. Mum thought about it, emphasising the word 'sofa' when she agreed. He was lying on it when I went down in the morning, fast asleep with his feet sticking out over the end. I looked down at him, and then at his picture on the mantelpiece, thinking how I'd done the same with Veronique's Nanai. I'd been able to recognise her from the photograph, but I couldn't do that with Dad. I knew it was him but I couldn't make the two things connect up.

I still can't quite, though I try at weekends when he comes round to see me and take me out. Not every weekend because sometimes he's working. And sometimes he doesn't come, and it's not because he's working but because of other, complicated things, which he tells me about afterwards but which I can't quite get my head round. Mum just sighs when he doesn't come, shaking her head as she lowers the blind back down. She tells me that it's not because of his reasons.

'He's an actor,' she says, which apparently explains it.

'At least you actually have a dad now,' Bradley said, at school one morning.

'Two–one,' I told him, before running off to art therapy with Mr Prentice.

I see Mr Prentice every week now. Veronique's there of course, and Billy comes too now. He makes these big, clumpy clay things while I do pictures of babies, and then toddlers, and then five-year-olds and then only just ten-year-olds, all looking a lot like me (but not quite). Mr Prentice says they're really good but I'm not interested in what they look like to other people. For me it's about connections. Not making them, but finding the connections that are already there, seeing them amid the confusion of everything else. For instance, that dream I had about brown water. It wasn't about something that happened to me. It happened to Antony. It was the last thing he ever knew, but I had the dream because I'm connected to him. I'm connected to him forever, and not just him, either – Billy, for instance, who I thought I hated; I'm connected to him by things we have in common and these are stronger than the things that made us hate each other. And not just Billy, either, but everyone, everywhere, is connected if you can just see how, like Veronique can. It occurred to me while I watched her build her DNA model that the reason she smells like somebody somewhere is eating candyfloss is obvious. It's because somebody somewhere *is*.

And Mum's making connections too. Or not trying to ignore them any more. She sees Dr Mara one hour every week for a chat, but it's her painting that really helps. She brought all the pictures from her bedroom down to the kitchen and I watch her, every night, as she fills them in. The middle, where she lost Antony, the dips and the swirls of the angry water that took him away.

The water. The race!

I drove on, pushing through the blue shimmers and the bubbles, confused when – YES! – I got to the far end, because the loud thumpy noise hadn't stopped. When I lifted my head out and saw the man in the red shirt the noise carried on, and I couldn't understand until I climbed out and saw my schoolfriends, my mum, all the parents and teachers, Miss Phillips most of all, cheering. I thought for a second I'd won – until I saw all the other kids in their towels. I'd come SO last, but I didn't care. It was incredible, amazing, the best moment of my life – until I panicked.

But my swimming trunks were ON.

And that's it, just about, though I should probably tell you about the party. Veronique's mum and dad had it at their house after the swimming today, and the first thing I did when I got there was run to the bottom of their garden. Nanai was asleep and so I pushed the door open quietly, tiptoeing round to the wall. But I was disappointed: the photo was gone. I thought Veronique must have taken it and I was about to tiptoe out when I saw it. Nanai had it. It was face down on her lap and I picked it up, staring at Thu for a second before Nanai stirred and looked at me. I didn't know what to do so I just smiled at her, and handed her the picture, watching as she held it to her chest and settled down again, her wrist not quite covering Thu, who smiled out at me from the shadow of her mother's straw hat.

I smiled back, until Nanai fell asleep again. Back in

the house, Bradley told me he was being Lance again.

'But why?' I asked. 'What's wrong with Bradley?' Lance just shook his head and told me not to ask.

I told him fine, and then hesitated.

'I've got the same sort of news,' I said.

'Really? You mean you're not . . .?'

'Cymbeline Igloo? No,' I said, and I told him what Mum had told me. Igloo wasn't my real name! It was just one my dad took on to make him stand out more as an actor.

'He chose it because it was my brother's first word. He just came out with it one day. That's why Mum kept it.'

'Wow,' Lance said, before grimacing. 'So what should you be called?'

'Smith,' I said. 'Can you believe it?'

Lance said no and asked if I was going to change to that. I shook my head. 'Nah. I'm not going to worry about it. Igloo's my name now. And you don't have to worry about that other Lance. Lance is just you; it doesn't go anywhere else. And you can be any kind of Lance you want,' I added. 'Starting with my best friend.'

'Better best friend.'

I smiled because he was right. After what we'd been through we would be better friends. We knew what it was like to ruin it and so we'd make it stronger instead.

Uncle Chris came in then. He was really happy because he'd given up his job (even though we'd saved it for him). He announced to everyone that he was 'taking a strategic lateral movement' into something called 'ethical long-term investment potential' and that Alisha was going to help him.

Auntie Mill in came with him and she had an announcement too: she'd given up tennis and would be moving back home. Juni and Clay were SO happy, wrapping their arms round her and trying not to cry. I was happy too of course, though I had (and I still have), serious worries about her backhand.

We all went outside to play football and everyone beat their kick-up record. Even Veronique beat hers (two). Back inside she said she wanted to ask me something.

'Kissing,' she said.

I stared at her. *Everyone* stared at her. 'Er . . .?'

'Dad gave me this book about puberty and it's in there.'

'Right. So . . .?'

'Have you ever kissed anyone?'

'He's kissed me,' Mum said.

'Apart from her. Like, for instance, a *girl*?'

Everyone was still staring. Billy elbowed me in the ribs. He hasn't stopped doing that. 'Go on, Cym, *answer*.'

'No,' I said.

'Well, I haven't kissed a boy either. So would you like to kiss me?'

'Er.'

'Go on, Cym, *answer*.'

'Would I . . .?'

'Not now of course.'

'Not . . .?'

'Now. My body has yet to produce any progesterone. The book says I might start feeling like kissing a boy when I'm eleven. Year Six. What do you think? I mean, if I *do* feel like doing that then?'

'Well, Cym?'

'Fine.'

'Good,' said Veronique, 'because that gives you plenty of time to read about how to do it, doesn't it?'

I said yes and everyone laughed, apart from Mum.

She looked a bit nervous and it wasn't anything to do with what Veronique had said. I thought it was just stress from the pool, but it wasn't. When the doorbell rang she ran over to it like she was on fire, even though it wasn't her house. When she opened it I was surprised – because the man was there. The man who always comes with his little girls to her Sunday workshops at the National Gallery. I didn't know why he was there, but I did realise then that Mum had her dress on, the one she'd got from Oxfam. I was glad she was wearing it because who cares who it used to belong to, it was hers now, and she looked great in it. The man must have thought so too because he told her that over and over again.

Stefan. Mum told me his name when she brought him over. He had his little girls with him and the younger one grabbed hold of my leg. I pretended to mind but she was cute, actually. She had this unicorn with her called Silver, which got me thinking about the very last thing I have to tell you. The thing I couldn't tell you before because it hurts too much. And which I've been leaving to last, like tidying your room, putting anything before doing that. I so don't want to tell you it even now, but I have to, I know it, or the picture I've been painting won't be finished. It won't be real, will it?

I'd stared at them.

Once I'd got over the little hill.

My soaking, shivering Mum, being held by the man from the mantelpiece. Loads of people came rushing up. The picnic people, Lance's dad-dad, Veronique, Billy and Lance, and Auntie Mill too, hugging Mum and crying that she loved her as my dad held out his hand to me. I wanted to take it and I didn't want to at the same time, stepping backwards because it was all *too weird*. Which is when I saw him.

I just caught a glance of him, out of the corner of my eye.

Mum must have taken him in with her. I hadn't realised that, but she had. And she must have let him go – because he was there. He was in the shallower bit, where the current wasn't very strong. He was moving around in a circle, and there was a second when I might have been able to jump in and grab him. I often think of that moment. I probably always will. But I was too slow. I didn't take it and all I could do was watch as he turned round in the water, staring up at me with his big eyes, his ears spread out behind his head as he was sucked towards the middle. And then he slipped, and turned away, and there was nothing I could do, nothing but watch, my heart thumping, as Mr Fluffy tumbled, then disappeared, carried off by the rushing water.

THE EN—

OH NO – WAIT.

I haven't told you about Marcus Breen, have I?

Well, he was very quiet at the pool today. To start with. *Very* un-Marcus Breen-like. But once the cheering died down, and I'd been hugged by *everyone*, we all gathered at the other end of the pool where Miss Phillips had to count us. She did it twice, telling us to stay still, until her face went totally white.

'Marcus!' she said. 'Where *is* he?'

We panicked, everyone staring around at the seats and the fire exit and down into the water, until Lance shoved his armpit in my face. He was pointing up – at the diving board. The *really high* one. At a figure up there. A tiny white figure who was . . . naked!

'Look at me!' Marcus shouted, and we all did.

Everyone, all the parents and swimmers and everyone in the whole pool. 'Look at me!' he screamed again.

'I'M CYMBELINE!'

And then he leapt off the board, waggling his legs as he flew through the huge expanse of bright, clean air.

As for Mr Fluffy, I've been thinking a bit more about him and I've realised something. He's, well, with Antony now, isn't he, which is where he belongs. And I'm with Mum, and Dad perhaps, and Lance and Veronique, and even Billy Lee.

Which is where I belong too.

THE END